TRANSCENDENCE: AN ANTHOLOGY OF HUMAN THOUGHT

A collection of short stories, poems and missives about

Decision-Making for Good or Bad

Contributing Writers from Australia, Canada, China, Finland, India, Jamaica, Pakistan, Philippines, United Kingdom, & United States.

Works are edited maintaining spellings appropriate for the origin country.

www.trode.ca

ISBN 13: 978-0-9947408-7-8

The Earth is host to billions of creatures called Homo sapiens. We fancy ourselves a rather clever lot. Our brains are large relative to most other animals', so why is it that humans are constantly making choices with deleterious outcomes? Indeed, we humans are capable of beautiful things, but what is it that leads us to make such curious choices? This anthology is dedicated to the reasoning, motivation, and execution of human decision making.

TABLE OF CONTENTS

Preface
Benoit Chartier
Editor and Publisher

Transcendence: An Anthology of Human Thought. That's quite the fancy title. What does it mean? The latter is fairly straightforward. The former, though, takes a bit of explaining. For that, we need to go back to the genesis of this anthology.

At its origins, the anthology is a collection of short stories concocted by a group of authors belonging to an invite-only author's group called 'Ramao's Oasis'. Its denizens are the mutineers and stowaways from another group, whose name shall not be spoken here.

One of the administrators for Ramao's Oasis one day proposed we should create an anthology, to which many of us agreed. We each sent in a story, and watched as it came together, like a well-crafted vase. Each of us adding our own clay and design.

A few days before the whole manuscript was to be uploaded to the web for publication, it was announced to us that Josh, the inceptor, had disappeared. Not simply from the group, but from the face of the Earth, as well. After investigation, we discovered that Josh Jones was not his real name. That he had disappeared before. Our vase felt as if it were falling to the ground.

Evidence suggests that Josh was not in complete control, and that his troubles were psychological, and not criminal. To this day, we do not know where he went.

All this said and done, we were left with a quandary: what to do with the anthology. We decided, after having put it to a vote, to publish under this imprint (Of which, for the sake of full disclosure, I am the sole proprietor).

To a certain degree, transcendence means to find good in the bad and make something better of it. Having had this roadblock put in our collective path meant that we had to overcome, which, so far, we have. Our work of art will only shine brighter for the fires it has been put through.

The authors which comprise this anthology, and the group itself, come from a great many countries. This is something which adds value to the stories, since we've gone beyond the traditional national boundaries to create something interesting. There again, you have transcendence.

Lastly, in my experience, everyone involved in this project has come together to create something full of meaning, to share with the world, and perhaps find truth, or beauty, in narratives that they wish others to discover. That, to me, is another form of transcendence.

I hope you enjoy the hard work that these authors brought to the table. That you see in them your own truths, and perhaps, see transcendence in daily life because of them.

Benoit Chartier, Editor

An Introduction of Sorts
Jai Thoolen
38 years old, Australian legend and famous comedian to be.

LEFT OR RIGHT

If I get to the end of a path and I have a choice between left and right— I'd start digging. Or go back the way I came. Or maybe sit on the spot and wait, indefinitely. Conformity doesn't look right on me. I do not wear it well. I put on my rebellious pants and I rebel.

I have a theory that there's always more treasure to the left. Like, left always turns (pardon the pun) out better. This can't possibly work as often as I would like to think. I've done no research and collected no data on the subject, but it's something that makes me happy to pretend to believe.

I don't like being forced into decisions by the lack of choices. I want to choose from an abundance of options so that I feel like I haven't been manoeuvred or corralled. I don't want to be one of 'those', I want to be ME, leading the way. Or, if it can be arranged, could I be first to go? That way, I'm forging the path, right? Wait! Who made the path? Who gave us these choices? Someone's been there before by default. Maybe if it's an overgrown path I could claim I blazed— a pre-loved trail or something? There are not many places on Earth that haven't been blazed, I guess. That doesn't leave me much to do. New worlds perhaps? The centre of the Earth? Some hidden jungle in far reaches of who-knows-where? Been done, most likely.

You know what… fuck it, I'll go left!

Squatter
Tom Ashton

Gerald lived at Number 4, Green Lane, Grenton Village, Cumbria, in a small cottage coined 'The Green House', not merely because of its window sills and doors, perpetually gleaming with a fresh, green gloss, but also because of its garden which could easily have been labelled an 'Area of Outstanding Natural Beauty', with every perennial plant and effervescent flower clearly clipped, and watered, with ultimate care and precision. This made the pavement outside of Number 4 a regular social rendezvous for the villagers, an arrangement which Gerald regularly and loudly communicated his disapproval of. This non-communal behaviour of Gerald's gained him the disfavour of the other villagers, which sat just fine with him as he didn't want to speak to them anyhow. However, there was one woman, Mrs Summers, wife of the area's Police Constable, who refused to observe this hostile agreement and regularly expressed interest in his well-being, under the guise of scratching his Jack Russel, Bert, behind the ear.

Photo by Ibrahim Rifath on Unsplash

"Can't you mind your own damn business?" he'd ask her.

"No one's business is their own in Grenton, Gerald!" She'd laugh in reply.

On one sunny Sunday, following this disconcerting exchange, he noticed Mrs Smith, Mrs Higgins, and Dr Parker grouped together by the street sign, and instantly concluded that they were evaluating his verbal reproach of Bert for encouraging Mrs Summers, although a further glower revealed that their attention had been claimed by the middle-aged stranger, standing outside Number 3. The house was the shame of the street, a dilapidated two-up, two-down which the council refused to deal with, despite the constant barrage of letters they received from the villagers. This skinhead, in his black plastic jacket, and stained grey joggers, turned to look at Gerald as he past.

"Anyone living here, mate?"

Gerald sniffed and continued past.

"Whatever!" The man said and threw his shoulder against the door, drawing a melodramatic shriek from Mrs Smith. Gerald looked back as the door to Number 3 swung shut. It's rusty brass knocker, bouncing softly upon its chipped, red canvas.

Gerald and Bert finished their lap of the village and returned to Green Lane in time to witness PC Summers walking carefully up the path towards Number 3, with Mrs Smith, Mrs Higgins and Dr Parker still bearing witness from the security of the street sign. He took up the knocker, brought it carefully down and waited. Nothing happened. Gerald felt himself slow reluctantly, just another nosy neighbour amongst a growing collective of nosy neighbours.

As Summers took up the knocker again, the door opened and a fist smashed him in the eye. Both Mrs Smith and Mrs Higgins shrieked this time, as the flapping copper fell sideways into the tangled, brambly mess of the lawn.

"That's what happens to people who knock on my door! Pig or no-pig!"

Then the Squatter went back inside and Mrs Summers appeared, to help her disorientated husband to his feet, whilst the neighbours buzzed.

Pounding dance music woke Gerald at 3 AM. He sat bolt upright and glared out into the street where Mrs Summers could be seen in her pink dressing gown and slippers, striding fiercely towards Number 3. Her husband stood in their living room window, watching, whilst simultaneously failing to calm their screaming child.

The irate woman pummeled the door for an age before the decibels eventually dropped and the Squatter emerged. She gestured towards her house and yelled inaudibly as he watched, seemingly unabashed, and then sprang upon her. They struggled briefly on the ground, him laughing, her screaming, until eventually he relinquished his grip and she wriggled free, weeping and wiping her lips on the back of her hand.

"Next time we go all the way, sweetheart!"

Gerald thinned his lips and stepped out of bed. He dressed himself in his usual chords and shirt, with a green cardigan for the night's breeze, if there was one, and then opened the top drawer of the dresser. From this drawer, he took a well-oiled, highly polished Beretta M9 and weighed it in his hand. A heavy weapon, though one which would never jam and would ground anything he fired at within fifty metres.

Gerald glanced towards the skeleton in his mirror, draped in folds of heavy elephant skin. Would he even be able to lift the gun? His eyelids closed, his ears tuned out the thumping bass, and his mind permitted access to the repressed memories of the thirty years he'd spent amassing his villain's pension in the East Midlands: Nottingham, Derby, Leicester... before he'd fled to Grenton a decade ago. Gerald's natural capabilities had remained with him and there was a chance that he was not yet too old to exercise them. He opened his eyes and found the gun aloft, at the end of an iron girder, elephant skin pulled taught. A coolness pulsed through his body, washing away any remaining anxiety.

Bert whined and followed him to the door.

"I'm sorry, Bert, I know I promised you... but this isn't for me."

He left Bert scratching at the door and stamped down the pavement towards Number 3. Adjacent windows blazed into life as one neighbour spotted him and then phoned another. He did not turn his head until he reached the Summers' place, where he took a moment to nod towards the sombre family, watching him from their living room window.

The door to Number 3 opened before he could knock.

"What do you want, old man?"

Gerald stopped a little ahead of him, nose wrinkling against the stench of alcohol and gingivitis.

"I've brought you something!" Gerald said and whipped an object from his pocket, causing his enemy to retreat a step.

"Take this, it's all I've got. Take it and get the hell out of here!"

He extended the wad of notes, which the Squatter accepted with a sneer, and tucked inside his pocket. Then, Gerald took a right hook to the face and fell heavily onto the concrete path with an audible crack. The gun skidded away out of reach.

"You gonna shoot me up, you old mug?"

Gerald felt a kick shatter a rib and he groaned involuntarily.

"Come on bruv, what you got?"

He felt his leg bruise.

"Leave him alone!"

The Squatter and Gerald looked around to see Mrs Summers standing there, before the whole village, with the gun in one hand and her baby in the other. The Squatter laughed and said, "You aint got it in you, love... But I've got something you can have in you!" He rubbed his groin.

"Come on, Pauline," said PC Summers, putting a hand on the gun. "This isn't the way."

"That's right, Pauline, listen to your girlfriend!" He mocked, gesturing towards PC Summers, as the crowd moved in to shield Mrs Summers and her baby. PC Summers looked at him, through the eye that wasn't blacked, and said, "the baby's not old enough to see how the village deals with troublesome outsiders…yet." Then, with a sharp crack, he gave the red door of Number 3 a fresh coat of paint. There were no screams.

When Gerald returned from hospital the following week, he was delighted to encounter the same hostile indifference from the neighbours to which he'd grown accustomed, except for Mrs Summers of course, who approached him smiling, with Bert on a lead and a plastic bag containing a wad of cash and a heavy object wrapped in an orange tea-towel.

"How are you, Gerald?"

"Can't you mind your own damn business?"

The rest of Grenton Village never pried into Gerald's business or history, a favour he was more than happy to reciprocate. The people only ever showed interest in his garden, which bloomed brighter than ever that year, particularly the roses, on soil which had been considerately turned in Gerald's brief absence. Another practice, which would forever remain undiscussed by mutual unspoken agreement.

Photo by Ellen Carlson on Unsplash

As the Crow Flies
Randall Thompson

The year that I turned thirteen stands out in my mind, even now that I am middle-aged. We didn't have the internet, or video games, or even much television to speak of back then, that would be in 1977. Just three channels and two of them were the same, most of the time. We had books though, great books. Robinson Crusoe, the adventures of Tom Sawyer and Huck Finn. Even Jules Verne and of course The Hardy Boys. Of the little television we did have, my favorite was the Wonderful World of Disney on Sunday nights. I remember my brother Graham and I rushing through our chores after supper so we wouldn't miss a minute.

Our family lived on a farm in one of the northern States, though we only had a handful of cows and an old horse. Pa worked on a logging crew, so there wasn't much time for farming anymore. My brother and me was too young yet to work the farm: that was apart from tending our old milk-cow, Bessy, and chopping firewood. Graham was three years older; he was going to be a logger too. At least that's what he said all the time.

One night, I remember Pa coming home later than usual, we had just gone to bed. I remember hearing Mom asking if they'd found him… Billy.

"What are they talking about?" I asked my brother, waking him. We slept in the same bedroom just at the top of the stairs.

"Yes, and not a minute too soon. Billy just about made it to the bog this time—," I heard Pa say.

"The bog? What's that?" I asked.

"A swamp, idiot," replied my brother as he hugged his pillow.

"Why was he heading to the swamp?"

"Cause he's retarded, doe-head. Now, go to sleep."

It was later that year, I suppose after the winter that I heard about this bog and Billy Williamson again. I was sitting in the old rocking chair beside the wood stove – rocking for all I was worth. Mom had warned me to cut it out once already. I suppose

I was bored or waiting on my brother for something, when Pa came in from the back porch. He went straight to the cellar door and took down his rifle that always hung above.

"What's that for?" Mom asked him.

"Going back in the woods—again." That was all that he said as he pulled on his raincoat. I remember a strange look passing between them.

"Did Billy go in the direction of the bog this time?" asked Mom. Her tone was low. I wasn't used her hearing her talk to Pa that way.

"Haven't picked up any tracks yet—the fields are so wet that run towards the lake." Pa glanced over at my brother and me. "But that's where we're searching again today."

It was springtime, but just. The ground was slushy, the mud in the driveway was spongy. Graham said that was on account of the frost coming out.

My brother and I went to the front step and stood there watching Pa drive out the lane in the old Ford and turn towards town. "Is it very far?" I asked. My brother was annoyed that Pa hadn't let him go along, since Graham nearly always did go these days, no matter where Pa was heading to.

"What is?"

"The bog?"

"Pa said it's the other side of town, then down Mt. Dixon Road." I searched my memory, I couldn't place it.

"Sounds far enough."

"Far enough for what, doe-head?" my brother asked in a condescending tone.

"Far enough from here… he won't come this way." I didn't know much about Billy… Billy Williamson. Just that he wasn't right in the head and that from time to time, he ran away and sometimes all the men around the neighborhood had to go help find him. My brother quirked a smile and placed his hand on my shoulder, steering me back inside the house. He pushed me towards the kitchen, then to the back door and out onto the back step that looked down over our long fields to the woods beyond. Graham pointed his finger towards the immense forest.

"It's over there someplace."

"But I thought you said it was on the other side of town," I said, knowing that town was in a much different direction.

"I did doe-head, but then down the Mt. Dixon road—a long way, and that puts you in that area over there some place."

Behind our house, in fact behind all the farms on our road that ran between the two towns of Birchwood and Elm Valley, behind all that was a vast forested area. I would learn years later that our property only ran for about a mile from the road in front of our house into the woods. But beyond that was government land, and that took up thousands of acres of forest and ran all the ways to the old Interstate and the farms that were parceled out along that road. Then to the west and the north the woods ran all the way to Elm Valley, some twenty miles away. To the east, the woods ran towards Mt. Dixon road and beyond it to Lake Kilarney. Although I didn't understand much about all this geography that my brother was now lecturing me on, I did know one thing—Lake Kilarney was surrounded by the bog everyone was talking about.

"You see, doe-head, it's not that far… as the crow flies."

My brother's description gripped me. "What do you mean… as the crow flies?"

"On the road it might take twenty minutes in the old Ford but there—see…" and he pointed to a bird, not a crow necessarily, but a black bird nonetheless. "That bird could fly in a straight line over all them trees and be there in about five minutes."

I must have had an unconvincing expression on my face. "Or to put it another way… Billy Williamson could come through the woods in this

Photo by Sydney Rae on Unsplash

direction." Graham pointed his finger down at the stone we were standing on. My eyes followed—my heart pounded. "Pa said it wouldn't be much more than eight or nine miles… as the crow flies." A shudder went up my back and the hair stood up on my neck. I stared back towards the sweeping view from our back-yard across the long fields to the forest that lay beyond. The hay fields were still streaked with melting snow and slush. Patches of ruddy brown grass and matted clumps of dead weeds stuck out everywhere. The hardwood trees were still bare; the day was grey. It wasn't raining but it wasn't far off, an icy fog obscured the horizon. My face was cold. My brother left me and went back inside. I stood there contemplating the possibility that Billy hadn't gone for the bog—that he hadn't followed the same route that apparently, he had in the past. Every other time when he ran away… when the men along with his father had found him– had caught him. Every other time he went in the other direction. Maybe this time he changed his tactics even though he was handicapped, assuming that he didn't want to get caught and brought back home. Maybe this time, he had decided he was going to do it differently. Perhaps this time, he thought it out more or maybe had saw something that made him think about it in another way. Maybe this time, he would come this direction… maybe this time he would go as the crow flies.

Normally, I kept myself busy with my own thoughts. I'd be playing with my dinky cars or out in the slush with the Tonka grader I had gotten for

Christmas two years earlier. Maybe I'd be coloring or drawing pictures. I was good at that– at drawing and stuff. Or I'd be watching TV. At least when I could get a station that I liked. The Flintstones were on just before supper and right after Bewitched. But then I'd have the wood to get and before I knew it I had to get a bath and then bed so I wouldn't be a pain to get up before school. Mom really hated it when I was hard to get up. Over the next three days, I hung around the kitchen when Pa got home. I made like I was doing stuff with the box of newspapers but really, I was listening.

"This is going on too long, isn't it David?" Mom asked. I could tell by her tone of voice she was anxious. Pa had sat down at the table and was about to have the plate mom had put up for him after we had eaten earlier.

"About two days too long, now." I noticed a look pass between them. "We had over forty men in the woods today," he looked up at her. "Nothing."

"No signs? There was nothing left behind this time?"

"Nope. Billy always left a trail before… but not this time. No tracks neither."

"Isn't that odd. Why wouldn't there be any tracks? There's still some snow around–must be, in the woods, isn't there?"

"It's wet in the woods… very wet. Frost is out." Pa took a few mouthfuls and paused to take a drink of the hot tea Mom had just sat in front of him. She glanced at me across the room. I carried on rolling the papers into tubes, making out like I wasn't paying one bit of mind to their conversation. She sat at the table, leaned in slightly.

"Did he get as far as the bog this time?"

Pa looked up at her, glanced at me before replying. "There aren't any tracks but there isn't much ice left around the bog either… he may have."

"Oh dear." I could tell from my mother's tone that getting to the bog was not a good prospect, though I wasn't sure why.

"If'n he got in there—," my father said between mouthfuls of potatoes and gravy. My mother was quiet now. Pa took the last spoonful of supper and

sat back in his chair. He took a mouthful of tea and wiped his mouth with the back of his hand. It was then that I noticed that his clothes were mostly wet. He looked chilled right through to the bone as mom would say. I could tell she was sizing up Pa's attitude. Her expression was grim.

"What is his obsession with the bog, David?" asked Mom.

"Don't know–his father won't say. Doesn't say much about Billy, 'bout why he runs."

"Evelyn says Billy has the mind of an 8-year-old."

"Well, even an 8-year-old should know better than to run into the woods and hide for days on end."

"Poor boy–he must be very hungry," said Mom, her expression was filled with concern as she glanced over at me. Maybe she was thinking about what if it was me out there… in the bog.

"He may not be that hungry…" Pa looked up at mom as he drank from the mug of tea. Mom stared at him.

"She's not putting food out, is she?" I stopped rolling the papers.

"She has before. I imagine that she is this time, too." There was several minutes of silence.

"Well, what else can she do–she is his mother, David." Pa pushed his chair back.

"It ain't encouraging him to come to any of us out looking for him–not if he's coming back at night and getting food his mother is leaving out behind the barn. Just making things worse–a lot worse."

"Are the men going out again tomorrow?" she asked.

Pa took another swill from the china mug. "Yup." He looked over at her, "Just one more day, I reckon."

"Oh–what about the dogs? You said that they were going to bring in the search dogs?" her voice rang with alarm. She had forgotten, I think, that I was still sitting on the floor in the pantry, digging through the papers in the wood box.

"They did already," he replied, "brought them in from Truro this morning–they got no scent of Billy– nothing."

"Oh dear, those poor people."

"It's too wet, I guess–just enough slush around to make tracking next to impossible." My father set down his empty cup. "They thought that they had a trail behind the house on this side around the wood pile and out to the barn of course, but Billy would have been all around there anyways. Nothing across the road in the field towards the lake… or the bog– nothing." Pa pushed back his chair and stood.

"But that's good… At least he may not have gone that way." Mom's tone lifted slightly–there was a trace of hope now.

"Well, it's been ten days now and that's too long to…" Pa caught himself, he glanced over at me and then back to mom. He just nodded to her. His expression was sallow. He didn't need to say anything more.

"I see." Mom got up too and crossed the kitchen to the wood stove. She had some of Dad's clothes hung on the wire over the fire, warming. "Put these on, David–get out of those wet things." I looked up at Mom and she could see, I think, that I had been listening to their conversation. I must have had a look on my face. "And you have wood to get, Mister… don't need to be in here eavesdropping." I didn't know what she meant. I looked over at Pa–he winked, and I knew it was okay, but I got along to my chores just the same.

The next few days passed and the mood was grim. I remember a few of the neighbors coming by to visit after supper–after Pa got home from searching for Billy. It hadn't been just one more day as he had said, but several. Mom made a point to shoo me on my way out of the kitchen once talk turned to the search and dogs. I don't remember when it all ended, but it did. One day, Pa didn't take down the rifle from above the cellar door, didn't get in the truck and head out in the morning, not searching anyways. I heard him say something to my brother about getting back to work, log trucks coming, or something like that. All of a sudden there was no more talk about Billy or the search and there was no more mention of the bog.

I remember standing on the back step and looking down the fields. I don't know what I was looking for, but I became fascinated with watching the crows that summer. I marveled at how high they flew and how far they went. We had a lot of crows around the farm. Mom threw out the leftovers on the back lawn every morning, whatever the barn cats didn't get would be left for the crows. Every morning that summer I got up early to check on them.

Eventually, I forgot all about Billy Williamson. And I probably even forgot how I became interested in watching the crows. The summer came, and I was busy with my friends and all the activity on the farm. It was when we were getting the hay that August that my brother and I were on the wagon collecting bales of hay at the bottom of the long field that ran from the back of the barn to the woods, that we saw them.

"Look at all them Christmas trees doe-head." Graham was pointing to the edge of the woods not twenty feet from the wagon.

I loved Christmas, and the mention of it sent me straight into euphoria.

"Where?" I demanded, lunging to the far side of the wagon. We had paused for Pa to fix something on the old baler–that happened often. My brother jumped off the side of the wagon and I scrambled after him. Sometimes it annoyed him when I would go off after him, but he didn't seem to mind this time. We walked the short distance to the edge of the woods. And he was right, there were several trees about twice my height that looked just perfectly shaped for Christmas trees.

"That one's a beauty," I exclaimed grabbing on to one that was especially bushy.

"Not that one doe-head! That's a cat-piss spruce," retorted my know-it-all brother.

"A what?"

"Cat-piss spruce– smells like cat piss… Those ones are bushy, but they stink." I leaned in and smelled and whether it was just the power of my brother's suggestion or reality, but just then I recoiled, believing I had my face right in a bunch of cat pee.

"Gross!"

"These ones over here though–them are fir trees," directed my brother. I followed his lead and although they were a little less bushy than the cat-piss ones–still, they were formed with perfect rings of bows… just like the best shaped Christmas trees. My brother and I messed around the edge of the woods for a bit, selecting which one we would use for this coming Christmas. Pa always brought us to the woods to chop one down but last year my brother and I had come down by ourselves, Pa said that Graham was old enough to do it. We had brought one of the toboggans and got a pretty good one. I remember he didn't chop the one that I liked best, however–said it was too big. Anyways–it was okay, near as I can remember.

As Graham and I pointed out our favorites, I remember thinking to myself, it would be great when I was old enough to come alone–that way, I would be sure to get the tree that I liked best, and wouldn't have to go along with what my brother said.

Soon, my father called to us and we ran back to the wagon and resumed packing on the hay bales as they slowly bumped their way out of the back of

Photo by Alexander Sinn on Unsplash

the dusty old machine. We turned away from the woods and made our path back up the long field to the barnyard. I remember looking over my shoulder, marking the spot in my memory where my favorite Christmas tree had been.

The summer slowly faded, and school began again. I remember I was in Grade 6 that year. Tom Smith was my best friend–had been since his family had moved to Birchwood when I was in grade two. I remember telling him all about my summer and about all the adventures that I had had around the farm. In those days, summers seemed to go on forever and the time between seeing our friends from school since we got out in June was nearly a lifetime. We had both changed a lot. I'm sure Tom

had grown taller and I was practically a grownup… at least in my own mind.

Tom told me all about his summer too, and I remember us both complaining about our older siblings. Graham was sixteen now and had become a pain. Tom's sister Janice was a year older than him and bossy–at least according to Tom. So, griping about our elders, as my brother called himself now, was part and parcel of our everyday conversations.

"Well I'm not taking orders from my sister any-more–I can tell you that. Not now that I'm in grade six," declared Tom. I forget why he was so worked up, but his words left an impression. I didn't need Graham telling me what to do anymore either and so my attitude began to shift.

We had snow early that fall. I remember it clearly because we didn't have all the wood stacked in yet, even though it was November.

"For goodness sakes boys–will you hurry up with the last of the wood– your father wants to shut up the basement windows," demanded Mother, one evening. Graham got up from his chair in the living room and slapped me on the back of the head as he passed by.

"Come on doe-head," Graham ordered. The Flintstones had just come on the TV, and it was right then that I decided I wasn't taking bossing from him anymore. I looked down at the empty plastic mug that I had in my hands and without giving it a moment's thought I wound up and threw it at Graham. I had never been good at throwing, never had been good at any sports, and had certainly never reacted physically towards my older brother before. So, it was all the more inexplicable that the plastic cup had sailed up into the air just grazing the living room ceiling and came down squarely on the top of my brother's head. Thud!

"Jesus Christ!" yelped my brother in shock as he simultaneously whipped around and rubbed the top of his head. He was lunging towards me when Mom appeared in the doorway.

"What on Earth is going on in here!" she squealed. "What kind of language is that?" My brother's rage was mitigated only by fear of our Mother's wrath. Although Pa swore from time to time–it was never tolerated inside the house–never. "Where did you learn language like that, Mister?" Her tone was sharp, and he froze for the scolding. My brother hung his head, but his face was beet red. I was afraid but only a little. I should have been more, but I had stood up to him… likely for the first time. I had won this battle and I knew it. I got up and picked up my cup.

"Sorry Mom," I said with a put-on sheepishness.

"He threw it at me," snarled my brother, sulking.

"Apologize to your brother and go do you chores."

"Sorry," I mumbled as I slipped past Graham. He was standing in the middle of the room, his head still hung down, his hand still rubbing his scalp, his other clenched tightly in a fist. I stepped around him carefully.

"Faker," I thought to myself, but held my tongue.

Our mother stood just a few feet away with her hands still on her hips. Foreboding hung in the air. I realized that there would be punishment for Graham for swearing…. maybe even an early bedtime.

"You can go pile wood, and Graham throw it down the window hole–all of it," ordered Mother. "And no more fighting or the pair of you are getting an early bedtime for a week." Mom's threat seemed like a prison sentence. There would be no more disturbance.

I remember I went to the cellar and Graham got his coat on and went outside. For what seemed like hours, I had to dodge blocks of wood as he threw them down the window hole. I was careful not to get hit… I was certain that he was making no effort to miss me.

After that, Graham didn't hit me in the back of the head anymore, but he also didn't help me with my chores either. He had gained some measure of respect for me, and with that came a little independence. I didn't mind doing my own chores, not getting old Bessy, nor chopping the wood.

My birthday came around early in December and I turned thirteen and that was it… I was pretty much grown up now, at least that's how I saw it.

And that's probably why I thought that I could get the Christmas tree by myself that December. Although I wasn't thinking about Christmas or Christmas trees the night I hit my brother on the top of the head with the cup, that was when I decided. I know it was. Somewhere in the back of my mind that was the moment when I decided I would go by myself to pick out this year's Christmas tree.

My birthday had been on Friday. Mom made me a chocolate cake– my favorite, and I remember I found two quarters inside my piece of cake… that was a thing back then. Dimes, nickels and even a few quarters shoved into the side of the cake before the frosting went on. I was super lucky to get fifty cents that year. Anyhow, turning thirteen was a big deal for me. My brother and I had patched up our differences long before my birthday, but we had also begun to do things separately.

Mom had re-papered one of the spare bedrooms and now I had my own room. That was a huge accomplishment, I thought, though my brother seemed much happier even than I did.

Fresh snow fell that Saturday, the day after my birthday. All I could think about was getting the Christmas tree that I had spotted back in August. This year, I was going by myself. This year, I would take an axe and a toboggan and make the trek down the long field to the woods. This was the year–this time, I was doing it by myself.

Despite my new-found streak of independence, this decision to go get a tree wasn't announced to anyone. Even though I was resolved that I was doing it, still there was a hint of doubt in my mind if I would be permitted to go alone. I could just imagine Mom weighing the decision… just see Graham smirking with his arms folded waiting for mom to say– "your brother has to go with you." I could just see it all happening just like that. So, I kept my plan to myself. I would simply dress warmly as though I was going out to play and slip around behind the big barn.

I'd have to hide the axe inside my winter coat until I was out of sight of the kitchen window… just behind the horse barn. Then head down the field with the toboggan.

My plan was set. Sunday morning, I got up and had the porridge that Mom had cooked. I loved porridge, but we could only have it during the winter months. Mom said it would give us hives if we ate porridge in the summertime. I didn't understand that, but I believed her.

My only challenge was going to be getting away without Graham spotting me. So, I was super careful to not raise any suspicions.

After breakfast I got dressed and slipped outside. I wrapped up the axe and some rope in an old blanket that we used to sit on, and was just about to head out when my brother opened the door to the back porch.

"Where you headin' doe-head?"

I froze in my tracks. How I answered was going to make or break my plans. I didn't turn around, in a split second I decided to lie. I didn't often lie to my brother but in that moment, one came to my lips with amazing ease.

"Oh, I'm just going to play in the barnyard for a while… Why—do you want to play with me?" I don't think that I had asked my brother to join me since the incident with the head thumping a month before.

"Hardly," he scoffed and went back inside. I breathed a sigh of relief and resumed my adventure. First to the barn and then once out of sight, straight down the cow-lane towards the hayfield. There was a good 8 inches of snow on the ground. In some places it would hold my weight and the walking was easy, but once I reached the hayfield, about halfway to the woods, the snow was softer, and I plunged through with every step. By the time I reached the edge of the trees I was exhausted and had to set down on the toboggan for what seemed like a long time.

It felt strange being out there alone. The air was frosty. There was a slight breeze, and my face stung a little. There were a few flurries in the air, but it wasn't snowing. The weather didn't worry me. Looking back up the long fields to the house, I was suddenly aware of how hard it was going to be to drag a heavy tree back home even with the toboggan. For a moment I regretted not telling Graham what I had been planning to do.

"No one knows that I'm down here," I thought to myself. "That probably wasn't the best idea." I turned towards the trees. There was silence. No birds, no squirrels—nothing. It was much different than it had been in August. Back then there had been the rattle of the tractor and the whoosh of the bailer as its great plunger made its slow steady thump against the matted hay. And when we had been stopped and Graham and I had been picking out trees there had been birds at least… a chattering squirrel, even, and the sizzling of crickets.

I began to get a knot in my stomach. My mind raced, and I remembered stories I had seen watching the Wonderful World of Disney… shows with bears and wolves and mountain lions. I wondered for a moment if we even had mountain lions in this part of the world. But just before I allowed my imagination to run away with itself, I spied the top of a perfect tree.

"Geez… look at that!" I exclaimed. I pulled out the axe and made my way through a snow drift. I got right up to it… it was beautiful. Tall and straight and the lushest color of green–Christmas tree green. I chopped down an alder bush, so I could see the back side of it. Four, no five rings of bows… perfectly shaped with a perfect pointy top… just right to fit the angel that we always had on top of the tree. I was just about to start chopping when my brother's voice whispered inside my head: "cat piss spruce…"

I would never hear the end of it if this turned out to be one of those cat piss spruce trees. I stepped back and looked the tree over. "Was it too bushy?" I asked myself. I leaned in to smell… I wasn't sure. I took off my winter hat, and my scarf. I needed to get my whole face right in between the branches. Well, now I wasn't certain. The more I smelled it, the more I thought that it might be.

"God damn it!" I surprised myself, swearing out loud. I looked around. There was no one to hear me.

A crow cawed from somewhere close by. "Caw-caw-caw." It startled me. Suddenly and for no reason my mind snapped back to thoughts about Billy Williamson… he had never been found from back in the springtime when he had gone missing from his home in Mt. Dixon. The crow cawed again. "Caw-caw-caw…" "That was months ago," I thought to myself. An eternity– that had been still last school year when that happened. I tried to reassure myself. The crow cawed again.

"Shut up!" I yelled.

I think it cawed again. I looked for it, the crow. It was very close. Up one of the taller trees watching me.

"Stop it!"

I took a few steps further inside the woods, then a few more and a few more. The crow cawed again.

"Caw-caw-caw!"

"There you are!" I spied it. A large black crow was sitting out on a long dead limb, way up at the top of an old maple tree.

"Caw-caw-caw!" My stomach shivered. Something about the scene terrified me. I looked around: I had gone into the woods a ways—I could still see the field. I wasn't lost but a blanket of cold surrounded me. I could see my breath. My heart was pounding in my ears. The hairs stood up on the back of my neck. Slowly, I looked around away from the field, deep into the woods.

"Caw!"

I swung around with the axe and struck the old dead tree the crow was sitting in. I swung wildly another few times. I suppose I was trying to scare it into shutting up, if not flying away altogether. My blows did dislodge the noisy bird, but the thumping of the old dead tree had also shaken free the branch that the crow had been sitting on. I glanced skyward just in time to see the limb falling straight down on top of me.

I just remember the whack on the top of my head… I fell to the ground. I'm not sure if I went unconscious. My ears were ringing, my vision was blurry. I lost track of time and I felt cold laying in the snow at the base of the dead maple.

I'm not sure if I was awake but I became aware of someone else nearby. I heard movement in the trees behind me. Someone was standing over me, looking down. I opened and closed my eyes–I couldn't focus. A shiver ran through me. I tried to speak but words would not come. Then I felt myself being lifted, my left arm flopped down by my side, it felt strange, my body was limp. Graham wouldn't have done that. I could hear breathing, it was loud and there was a smell… a dampness, a little like the old dog when he was wet. Still I wasn't completely conscious. My head hurt but the ringing in my ears was fading.

I felt myself being laid on top of the toboggan–I could feel the rails beneath my back. I was waiting for Graham to say something–he was probably going to scold me. But he said nothing.

A little time passed, and my breathing returned to normal, I blinked, and my eyes cleared– I could focus again. I heard some movement in the snow just to my side, I turned my head.

I blinked several times as the image of a man dressed in dark clothing was moving away from me back in the direction of the woods.

In an instant, I realized that it was not my brother. I drew in my breath deeply to yell out–but I was too afraid to speak. The figure sank into the forest's edge. My eyes were frozen onto the dark image–he was tall, his clothes were raggedy, his head a mass of hair. He turned and at last I caught a glimpse of his face. His beard was so thick I only glimpsed his eyes.

I shut my own tightly–I didn't want to see anymore. Quickly I turned my head to the other side and held my eyes firmly shut, my whole body tensed–I barely breathed.

I have no idea how much time elapsed, but it was a long while as I laid there too frightened to open my eyes, too frightened to utter a sound.

"What the hell do you think you are doing… doe-head?"

The voice sounded far away at first.

"Doe-head… I asked you a question. What do you think you are doing?"

Finally, I came more fully awake. Apparently, I was still laying on the ground. My brother was looking down at me. He looked concerned. Suddenly I was aware of the pain in the top of my head and I rubbed it with my hand.

"Ouch!" My brother leaned down and reached his hand towards my head. I recoiled. "Don't touch it."

"Let me see doe-head!" Graham moved my hand away and very lightly touched my hair… it hurt.

Photo by Johannes Penioon Pexels

"Damn it, don't touch it."

"How'd you do that?" he asked.

"I don't …." Slowly, I began to remember the crow and yelling at it… an image replayed in my mind about the old dead tree. "A branch… it was a dead branch."

"So, you snuck down here and nearly got yourself killed by a deadfall…. Way to go doe-head." My brothers' condescending tone was strangely reassuring. I couldn't be hurt too badly then, I would be okay. "Got a good-looking tree though, by the looks of it."

Graham spoke as he always had – he was acting perfectly normal, he had seen nothing– perhaps I had dreamt it all.

I looked to my side, I was lying beside the toboggan now and a tree was tied up laying on it.

"Did you cut that down?" I asked.

My brother looked at me oddly. He cocked his head to one side.

"You did doe-head. Jesus, maybe you do have a concussion or something." I sat up and looked at him. Then back at the tree.

"Graham, I didn't cut down the tree– I hadn't gotten that far… there was this crow and the branch hit me… I didn't. I didn't get this tree." My brother just looked at me. I rubbed my head.

"Well then who did, doe-head?" he smirked. "Billy Williamson?"

Graham was smiling, kind of half-chuckling, but the longer he studied the expression on my face, the less he was grinning, the less he was smiling. He looked up and around behind us towards the woods. Graham walked over to the tree line. He was looking down at the ground, examining the marks in the snow.

"What is it?"

He didn't reply.

"What are you lookin' for?"

He didn't reply.

"Come on Joel… let's get you home." I think that might have been the first time he hadn't called me doe-head.

We didn't talk at all the whole time we walked through the snow up the hayfield and finally to the cow-lane and then the back of the barn. We made it to the barnyard and I collapsed – we both did.

"Why did you come looking for me?" I asked as we both lay there panting for air.

"I don't know– I knew you were lying to me this morning… just a feeling I guess." He paused. "Then there was this crow… just cawing its guts

20

out, kind of alarmed me. I guess I just went looking for you out behind the barn and saw your tracks."

Eventually, we got to our feet and trudged the rest of the way to the back steps. The snow clung to our coats. Our cheeks were rosy. I could smell the smoke from the woodstove in the kitchen. My stomach wasn't in knots anymore.

I touched my brothers' arm, stopping him from opening the porch door.

"It was him, Graham... it was Billy," my brother turned to me, I will never forget the look on his face. "A branch clubbed me on the head and I passed out. Billy carried me back to the toboggan and he must have chopped down the tree." Graham said nothing, but I knew that he believed me. His eyes left mine and swept back down over the long field we had just walked up from the woods.

"Don't ever do that again, Joel— don't go to the woods by yourself... okay?"

It wasn't just my brother's words, it was the expression on his face. I stared back at him, suddenly, I was aware that I was so cold, I was shaking.

"And don't tell nobody about ... Billy." My brother glanced back down the long windswept fields to the forest and nodded. "They'll have to go huntin' for him again," Graham looked back at me, his expression had become firm. "He doesn't want to be found, just let him be."

I nodded my agreement, though it would be years before I understood completely. I never did tell anyone about Billy and I never went back to the woods by myself.

Graham and I never talked about the incident again, we didn't even joke about it. So far as I can remember neither of us ever mentioned Billy Williamson ever again. That was 40 years ago, and Graham is gone now, died in a car accident last year. There have been stories over the years, about people seeing things in the woods— glimpses of a dark figure. Hunters hearing sounds like someone walking over branches, having the feeling of someone watching them.

I smile when I hear those stories. I recall my brother's instructions... "leave him be," I think to myself, "he doesn't want to be found."

Not Alone Anymore
Cyan Ciar

I stand on the edge of the curb and stare blankly at the passing traffic. My toes hang dangerously over the edge, and if I were to just step away from the safety of the sidewalk at just the right time, I could end everything so quickly… But I don't.

The yellow siding of a taxi pulls up in front of me, and it takes me a moment to remember that I had called one when I had first woken up. After a moment of hesitation, I finally climb in.

"So sorry for being late," the driver says, "but downtown traffic was terrible."

"You're okay," I reply.

"Now, where can I take you today?" The driver is smiling at me in the rearview mirror. Her eyes are so full of energy and her voice so light and carefree, that I actually envy her. I used to be like her, full of my own energy and not worried about a thing. Why can't I be like that again?

"Roaring Heights Cemetery," I say once I remember that she had asked me where I needed to go.

The driver nods and finally turns back to the road. "I can have you there in about ten minutes," she tells me.

"Take your time, I'm not in a rush right now," I tell her as I settle in for the short drive.

I stare out the window and replay my plan through my head until I remember that I promised to make dinner tonight. I sigh and shrug. Oh well,

I'll just have to fit it in quickly so that Yuko doesn't worry about it and catch onto my plan.

I'm about to rerun my plan once more when I'm interrupted by a familiar sight that brings back memories and sucks me in before I can stop it.

I feel excitement in my chest as we stand in line to buy our tickets. I hear my quieted footsteps as I get us a drink while you wait for the popcorn. The smell of cigarette smoke washes over me as we find our seats, because this theater still lets people smoke indoors. I taste the butter and popcorn melt on my tongue as we wait for the previews to end, and I can see you smile as I thank you for taking me out. I remember all of those things, even all of these years later, and I have to wonder, do you remember?

I gasp for breath as the squeal of car breaks bring me back to reality. We're stopped at a red light. I sink back into my seat and start to relax, but my eyes land on something outside that brings back another wave of crushing memories.

I can feel the Sun warm my whole body and the force it takes to push me on the swing. I see other kids playing games like tag and baseball. I can smell the fresh cut grass from earlier that day and can hear you yelling at me that it's time to leave. I can taste the chocolate on my tongue from the ice cream you always bought me. I still remember all of those hours we spent playing, can you?

I continue to drown in my own mind until I hear someone talking to me. Are they talking to me, or am I just imagining it?

"Sir?" The voice is louder this time, clearer too. "Sir? Are you okay?"

I blink my eyes open and see that I'm staring at the bottom of the car door. My forehead is pressed against the window, and I know I have a red spot in the middle of my head the second I sit up. "I'm all right," I mumble, "just fell asleep."

I can tell by the look she's giving me that the driver doesn't believe me, but I don't care. "Well, all right," she says. "I just wanted to let you know that we made it."

I nod and open my wallet. I hand the girl fifty dollars even though my fare is less than twenty. "Keep the rest," I say as I climb out, closing the door and crossing the street before she can protest.

I stand at the gates and listen as the taxi drives off while I prepare myself for my last visit to this place as a living person.

My legs carry me through the gate and down the main path before I can talk myself out of it. I pass the first and second row before I come to the third, take a right, and go down to the end before I reach my last stop before home.

Tears well in my eyes the moment I see the headstone in front of me, and I'm useless to stop them. This will be me in a few days, just another casket in the ground and a block of stone for people to stare at.

"Hey, bro," I whisper, not even trying to hide the tremble in my voice like I normally do. "I won't be here long, I have some things to do at home, but I just wanted to let you know that I'll be seeing you later tonight. I've been thinking about this for months now, and I've finally made up my mind."

The wind chimes in front of me move together and make a loud noise with a passing breeze, and I know that Leo is talking to me. I shake my head after the chimes stop moving.

"I'm not changing my mind," I say. "You can't stop me, Yuko can't stop me, not even God could stop me right now."

The wind chimes speak once more, but softer this time, and for some reason, I start to cry harder. "It's been two years," I say. "Two years, and I'm just getting worse. I was doing good for a while, I mean, I was genuinely happy and actually wanted to live, but that's slipped away again, and I can't get it back.

I just want to be where you are, so we can play games and laugh at stupid things together, is that too much to ask. Is it?"

I stand and cry for longer than I should have, but I don't care anymore. What does it matter if I'm late making dinner, after tonight, I won't have to worry about anything because I'll be dead. The pain, the heartache, the depression and loneliness, all of it will be gone, and I won't have to worry about it anymore. Not anymore.

After a few minutes of breathing, I'm finally calm enough to leave Leo's grave without making a fool of myself out on the street. I go back up the row and take a left, passing more headstones and telling myself that that will be me soon.

"I thought I would find you here," a familiar voice says when I reach the gate.

"Yuko?"

Yuko smiles at me and my heart breaks on the inside. I'm going to miss his smile more than anything. It never fails to make me feel like everything will be alright in the end, but this time, it just makes me even more sad than before.

When I finally feel like my dam isn't going to break and spill my heart all over the ground, I say, "I thought you were at work."

"Jerry came in and said that the store was closing early for software updates, so I left without a second thought. I went home to surprise you, but you weren't there, and neither was your wallet, so that meant you either came here or went to the bookstore, and it seems that my first guess was correct."

I stare at him, not sure what to say. What am I going to do now? Yuko is off, which throws all of my plans into chaos. I mean, I can still do them, I just have to do more acting than I had first planned. Right, acting. That's easy.

I throw on my best smile and nod. "It usually is," I reply. "You've always been good at figuring me out."

Yuko chuckles, and for a moment, I feel my chest warm with happiness, but as quickly as it entered, it left once more. "So, shall we got home and have dinner?" he asks. "I brought home pizza to

23

celebrate my early release into the world."

I can't help the small laugh that escapes past my lips at his comment. We only eat pizza whenever Yuko gets off work early, and every time he does he makes it seem like he was released from jail, but the truth is, Yuko loves his job and wouldn't change it for the world.

"Yes, let's," I say, taking the hand that Yuko offers me and we begin the walk home.

As we walk, Yuko tells me about his day, and I simply nod and drop comments when they're need-ed. I'm busy thinking about the things I need to do after dinner to keep Yuko from finding me early and saving me, and the things I want to do before I go to be paying attention to everything that he's saying.

Dinner is done and over with quicker than I can blink, and despite my best efforts, Yuko makes me smile and even laugh a few times.

"I'm going to take a shower when we're done," I tell Yuko as we wash dishes. "It's been a couple days since my last one."

Yuko nods as he takes the plate I just finished washing and dries it before putting it away in the cabinet. "That's fine," he says, taking the next plate. "I think I might sit in the room and read, so you can find me there when you're done."

"All right." I shut off the sink, dry my hands, give Yuko a quick kiss, and make my way to the bed-room to gather my things. Everything is a blur in my mind the moment I step into the bedroom. I grab clothes and a towel as quickly as I can and run into the bathroom to start the water. My heart won't stop pounding in my ears, my hands won't stop shaking, I can't breathe right. I'm too wound up to do this, I'm not right.

I shake my head as I dive into the shower. "No, you have to do this," I tell myself. "If you don't, it'll just keep getting worse and worse until you do something that's way worse than this. Just finish your shower, dry off, change, and get it over with, that's all you have to do."

I sigh. "Yeah, okay," I reply to myself. "Just shower and get it over with, that's all. Nothing more, nothing less."

I repeat the last line over and over like a mantra. Nothing more, nothing less.

My shower is over and down with in less than five minutes, but for me, that's not unusual. I've always hated long showers, even when I was a kid, and even though I would get teased for it, no one ever complained too much because it meant that it left more hot water for them to use.

By the time I'm dressed and staring at myself in the mirror, I'm no longer sure if I can go through with this. I have one half of myself saying I should do it while the other half says I shouldn't.

"Oh, come on, what do you have to lose" my bad half tells me. "You're always depressed and hurting. You don't have a job, you don't have a car, you don't have a life. All you do is sleep and dream about things you could do if you weren't down all the time. What kind of life is that, just sitting around all the time, feeling bad about everything and dragging the only person who cares about you down with you. Yuko deserves someone who isn't so lazy and weak, he deserves someone better than you, so go on, go ahead and do it already, just end it all, right now."

"But what about Yuko?" my good half counters. "If you do this, he'll be lonely without you. He loves you and wouldn't that be putting him in the same position you're in now?"

I shake my head. "No, Yuko is strong," I say. "He's stronger than I am, and besides, if I'm gone, he'll be able to find someone who won't drag him down all the time."

"That's right," the bad part agrees. "You are weak, and you do drag him down all the time. How do you think he feels about that? Do you think he likes coming home to someone who's always de-pressed and suicidal, because I don't. Yuko would be much better off with someone who showed him more kindness and affection than you do."

"But you are kind," the good part argues, "and you do show affection. They aren't in showy or flashy ways, but you show that you love him, and he takes notice of it. Remember when you were mak-ing a cake for the first time for this birthday and you burnt it on accident?"

I nod slightly as the memory comes back to me. I had never baked before, and I wanted to make Yuko something special for this birthday, so I decided to make him cake. I left it in the oven too long and burnt it. Yuko came home right as it came out of the oven. He wasn't mad at me like I thought he would be, but instead, he offered to show me how to bake.

We had started to make everything again when he flicked flour at me, so I did it back, and from there it had turned into a giant food war. There was flour and and eggshells all over the floor, the counter was littered with yolks and egg whites, and Yuko and I were both covered in flour, eggs, sugar, and whatever else we had thrown at each other. It's one of my favorite memories.

"Don't you want to make more memories like that?" my good half asks. "Don't you want to be able to see Yuko smile and hear him laugh?"

"I do," I say, my voice cracking a bit as tears fill my eyes. "But I don't want to burden him with all of this bullshit that's in my head, I can't do that to him."

"But you can. Yuko cares about you and wants to help, so just go tell him what's going on and you'll feel better."

I want to tell Yuko so badly, but I don't want to hurt him. I want to die, but I want to live too. I want to be happy again so that Yuko can be happy and we can make good memories together, but I hurt too much to try to be happy and all I do is drown in my pain and cry. I'm too messed up to be around. I'm too closed off to love. I'm too scared to try anything new. I'm too depressed to get out of bed for more than a couple hours. I'm too -

"Jason, what's wrong? Why are you crying?" Yuko is standing in the doorway and the bathroom door is open. When did he even open it? I don't remember him coming in.

"Jason?" He takes a tentative step towards me. I see the concern in his eyes and I lose it.

"Yuko, I'm sorry," I say, tears falling before I can stop them. "I'm so sorry. All I do is drag you down.

I'm depressed and boring all the time, I cry over the dumbest stuff, you come home from work and only the dishes and laundry are done, maybe dinner if I can find the energy. You try and take me out to do something, but all I want to do is stay home and sleep. How do you put up with me everyday when you could easily leave and find someone so much better for you?"

While I had been babbling, Yuko had walked over and hugged me from behind. "I don't want to find someone else," he says, his forehead resting against the back of my head. "I love you Jason, that's the reason I 'put up' with you as you put it, and if anyone should be sorry, it's me. I know that you're struggling, and I try and help how I can by taking you out places, but it's not what you want, nor is it what you need."

My heart beats faster when he tells me that going out isn't what I need. Memories of my youth come at me from all angles and I start to panic. I can't go back to one of those places, I can't! It would kill me if I did.

"Please, don't send me back to one of those places!" I plead, turning around in Yuko's arms to look at him. "Please, I don't think I could bare going back there, I hate them."

"Hey, hey, calm down," Yuko says soothingly. "I'm not sending you back there, I promise. I'm sorry, I didn't mean to upset you, I just meant that going outside isn't what you needed."

I sigh and nod as I start to get angry at myself. Great, now I'm overreacting before he had a chance to explain himself, nice job.

"You aren't boring either," Yuko continues, "and you cry over things that upset you, and that's understandable. Depression isn't something that's easily overcome, especially by yourself, and when I come home and find that you've done things, I'm proud of you because that means you got up and did things even though I know it takes a lot of energy out of you. I'm proud of you. You get up everyday and you fight, and I know you don't see it that way, but I do. I love you Jason, and I know that these past couple of years without Leo has been hard on you, but just know that I care for you and I want to help you, I do."

Yuko's words hit home in a way I never thought they would, and I start to cry harder than before. All of this time, Yuko wasn't disappointed in me, he was proud of me, and I haven't been alone, I've just made myself feel that way.

He holds me tight, and for the first time, I realize how lucky I am to have him in my life. I'm not alone, and I never was. I'm not alone anymore, and I never will be again.

A Mother Killed and Burnt
Imran Khan Bhayo

Ali's hand shook so much he could hardly press the numbers. Beep. Beep. Beep. The dog was barking, which disturbed his flock of twenty sheep and set them bleating. He didn't know what to say.

Ring. Ring. "Hello." A calm, efficient voice answered the call.

"Help!" The distraught boy cried.

"This is—" the officer tried again.

The boy cut off his prepared speech with another flurry of anguished words, "God help me."

"This is 15 Office, Police Help Line," the officer rushed through his words.

"Help me please, police sir!"

"Who are you and what's the matter?" The officer said, sounding kinder.

"Sir, I'm a shepherd, Ali. I've seen a dead body, but Oh! God! It's burnt."

"Where?" the telephone operator asked.

"It's so awful!"

"You must tell me. Where are you?"

"In the forest of Musa," Ali cried. "Maybe five kilometers away from the Daren Bridge over the Paradise River."

"What is your father's name?" Jamal asked

"Sir, father's name is Ayaz Ahmed."

"Okay, this phone number is yours, also?"

"Yes sir."

"Police will be there within five minutes. The Station House Officer, or S.H.O, of the Paradise Police Station will call you. Don't leave the spot until police reach there."

"Okay, sir. But I'll walk to the road. I can't bear to look at her." Wiping sweat from his forehead, he shuffled toward the road mumbling, "Bilo, come here."

At Ali's whistle, the white and black dog ran swiftly to him and crouched by his master, twisting, wagging his tail and licking Ali's foot.

Ali bent to move his hand over Bilo's head then sat in the shadow of a cedar tree. Turning his back to the awful sight of the burnt corpse, he repeatedly looked at his phone, awaiting the next call. Bilo pushed his head into Ali's hand. Putting his phone away, Ali petted him and then hugged him.

The phone buzzed, startling him. He hurriedly took the phone from the side pocket of his Kameez and looked at the phone's screen but saw an unidentified number. Attending the call, he said in a low voice, "Hello." To talk loudly seemed somehow disrespectful to the body that had already suffered so much indignity.

"You're Ali, son of Ayaz Ahmed?" An unknown man politely asked.

"Yes, sir."

"I'm the S.H.O, Inspector Haider. We're near the Musa Forest. Where are you?"

"I'll come out of the forest and stand at the river bank of the Paradise, by the road."

"That's good, Ali." Haider said.

As he reached the bank of the wide river, its ribbon of green cutting through the tan and barren landscape stretching away beyond irrigated fields, he saw two white police cruisers coming toward him. Ali smoothed his clothes and removed the cotton kerchief from his head to show his face, taking his axe from his shoulder to stand solemnly.

"Are you Ali, the shepherd?" A young police officer in a blank uniform popped out of a police car and looked at him with serious eyes.

"Yes, sir, I'm Ali."

"How are you, Ali?" Shaking hands with Ali, he introduced himself, "I'm S.H.O. Haider. 15 Police Help Line." He looked beyond Ali into the forest. "Where is the burnt corpse?"

"I'm fine, sir. Thank you. Come, sir."

"It's good habit to inform quickly to us about bad things and crimes seen by you. You did well."

"It's my dog, Bilo, sir. Otherwise, I was unaware of this thing."

Ali led the way through trees. As they grew closer to the body Bilo began to whine and squeak. "Bilo, just sit and be quiet," said Ali, "These are our friends."

Bilo immediately sat and was quiet.

***

"Stop there, Ali," Haider said, grabbing Ali's shoulder and seriously scrutinizing the ground. "There are a couple of footprints made by people in shoes, while you're barefoot." Haider squatted near the tracks and said, "These aren't fresh." He pointed to one of them. "See, beetles have crawled across this footprint twice, and a jackal walked across this one. They only come out at night. Maybe they were made yesterday."

He stood and turned to Ali, "Have you seen someone here?"

"No, sir. I was busy with my sheep, taking them to drink on the river's bank. They were eating around those berry trees with me following them. Bilo's barking finally drew me to this spot. Leaving me and my sheep, he ran off here. When he barked so much, I came here and saw the burnt body that he'd not leave. I looked here and there, but there was not any other person, Haider sir."

Haider squatted beside the body, covering his nose with his handkerchief. "Oh God! Now, we begin to find the words for this burnt body of a woman. The story of a person." Haider said. "Oh, Lady! How did you come to this place and this horrible circumstance?"

"Sir, come here," Sadiq called. "We've got something!"

"What?" Haider asked, picking his way toward him.

"This plastic bottle smells of petrol, and there were footprints also." Sadiq said, pointing. "I think there are two persons, a man and a woman. See the larger and smaller footprints."

"Good work of team. The criminals brought her here, probably already dead, to burn and destroy all the evidence. Instead they handed us a major clue! Now, we'll look for where they bought the petrol."

"Yes sir, you're the intelligent officer particularly in the murder cases," Sadiq replied. "You'll find the criminal of this murder so soon."

"You are flattering me," Haider said seriously.

Sadiq asked seriously, "What next?"

"Go to the river bank and search for signs that a vehicle pulled to the side of the road. This dead body didn't come here by itself; it was brought here using a car or other vehicle."

"Maybe the last night or the early morning, all matters happened here. Now, time is 12:20 PM, and date is 11th December 2017. Note this for the file."

The head constable, Ghadi, approached them. "Sir, I've recorded the statement of Ali." "He wants to go. His sheep are impatient."

"Have you noted his phone number and address?" Haider asked Sadiq.

"Yes, yes, sir."

Haider directed Sadiq, "Soon, the ambulance will arrive. You transport this corpse to the hospital and conduct all required procedures. Then issue the breaking news to some channels and offer a reward. Now, I'm going to meet some informers about this case. I'm leaving Ghadi here with you. If you get any more evidence or information, call me."

***

Nasreen was sitting on the palm mat on the floor of their two-room house, sewing dresses to earn money, when Zahid flopped down his head in her lap. Her only child and the dearest love of her life said, "Oh, my dear Amma! I want to study at the university to get the best education, not only for my life, but also yours. I want to be rich like Bill Gates."

Nasreen laughed and asked, "What is Bill Gates?"

"Oh mother! It's not 'What' but 'Who.' He is the richest man. He is Karon, whose treasuries' keys on the back of 100 camels. He's the lord of golden mountains."

"So, you want to be a rich man."

"Yes, Amma."

Nasreen smiled and kissed his forehead. "Zahid, you're my beautiful love whom I'll not lose. As a mother, it is not just my love, beloved son, but my responsibility to look after you as a teacher, a friend and a guider. I sacrificed my youth to save your dream, because you're my star that one day will shine on me. I starve for your dream in hope that one day you'll be my strong stick in my old age.

She caressed his silky brown hair. "Your father left you and me in this world when you were five years old. He always dreamed as you do now. He wanted all things as you do now. If I was educated,

28

then I'd not see this black snake of poverty today. Now I've no fear of this black snake, but I don't want this to be your future, Zahid.

Nasreen's house was a small one. It was also a hundred paces away from the village of Musa. Two rooms, a corridor and kitchen. No adjoining brick walls, but some wooden trunks erected to keep out the forest animals. The bathroom was thirty paces away, across a sandy and stony area. Water came from a spring that was two kilometers away.

Nasreen got up early every morning. She rode her donkey cart and brought water for her house. Then she milked her sheep and prepared tea for herself and Zahir. She went to some houses and did chores there. As she was sweeping the houses, washing pots and clothes, for which she received bread, rice and some vegetables from the owners of the houses. When finished with her chores, she brought the food to her house where she warmed it.

She looked into her son's blue eyes. "I'm behind you, Zahid. I've saved some jewelry for your marriage that was gifted by your father. I'll sell my jewelry and will work in a couple houses for your study. "What you read and learn I don't know, as I'm an uneducated woman, so you apply for admission at the university you like."

"Oh, mother. You're my dear mother. I'll do all I can for you." Zahid hugged his mother and ran happily out of the house to tell his friend that he'd get admission to the university.

His mother called, "Hey, Zahid, have your meal then go out." But he didn't reply. Nasreen laughed at the pleasure on his face and murmured to herself, "My longing is only to see you happy all the time. It is the joy of my life. You are the diamond of my life."

Nasreen sold her jewelry—a beautiful necklace her husband had slipped on as he kissed her where it hung. She also sold earrings that had been given to her by her mother when she married. The two sheep that had been bought to supply milk for her son were also for sale, and she also sold four silver bangles she always wore on her right arm. Lastly, she had some money saved for the difficult times and needs of life.

Within a couple months, Zahid gained admission in the Engineering University of Daren District. It was two hundred kilometers away from the village of Musa, where there were over fifty houses belonging to different families. Before going to the university, Zahid asked for some more money because he wanted to buy new clothes and shoes. He didn't want to wear old ones.

Nasreen was distraught, but she said to Zahid, "Wait here, I'll borrow where I work." For the need of her son and for his happiness, she went to one old lady, Javeeriya, who always helped Nasreen. Nasreen told about her son's admission to the university and her dreams and needs. Javeeriya agreed to help Nasreen.

"On one condition, I'll lend you money," Javeeriya smiled and said. "You'll not pay back from your own salary, but when your son finishes his studies and gets a good job, then he can reimburse me from that. The other condition is that when you need more for your son's study, you'll ask for it."

Nasreen gladly kissed her hands and promised, "Yes, I'll do as you ask."

Getting the money her son needed, she walked to her house. Upon arriving, she gave it to her son, hugging and kissing him.

For his farewell, she came with him at the main road, carrying his bag in her own hands and expecting some good not just for her son, but for her own future as well.

Zahid repeatedly said, "Mother, go back home. I'll go and wait for the bus on the road."

She smiled and said, "When you're sitting on the bus, then I'll go home."

After waiting some time, the green-striped bus arrived. He took his seat as Nasreen waved her hands at the departing bus, and he went happily away to the university. She went back to her house, which felt so empty without her son.

***

In the evening, Zahid reached the boys' hostel. He found his room and met his roommate, Ahmed, set his books down, and put his clothes in the cupboard.

After Ahmed had showered, he said, "Zahid, you have a bath, and then we can go to the canteen for dinner."

Nodding, Zahid took his towel and soap and entered the bathroom. He was startled at the sight of blue bordered white tiles, a steel shower, and faucets. In his house, he showered with water brought by his mother from the spring, stored in a plastic bucket. There was never as much water in his house as now flowed from that shower.

Zahid enjoyed showering more than he expected. Cheerfully, he dressed in new pants and shirt, and then they both went to the hostel's canteen. They talked to other new students, ate dinner together, and paid their bills separately. After their meal, they went back to their room and slept.

The first appearance in his classroom, he sat in a chair on the edge of the room. Within ten minutes, the whole place was filled with beautiful girls and handsome guys. Everyone else introduced themselves to the students sitting near them.

"Hi, I'm Zahid Malak."

"Hi, I'm Alisha." She was blonde and beautiful; a princess in the college classroom.

The professor came into the class, and after a short introduction, he started teaching the first period of Mathematics. Zahid was intelligent and interested in that subject. He asked and solved some question sensibly. Alisha befriended him. They sat together in class, went to the canteen or sports grounds together, and in the evening studied late in the library.

The librarian had to remind them several times it was closing time.

Zahid wanted to be with her every moment of the day. What Alisha asked or said, he immediately did without any objection, and she for him. Instead of saying they were in love, they'd read love poems to each other.

After a couple months, she invited him to her room. Alisha brought him a cup of tea.

Taking the cup of tea, he said, "Thank you dear Alisha."

For the first time, she winked and said, "I love you my dear Zahid."

Zahid sipped tea and silently pondered her, and she also looked at him. As they finished tea, keeping cups by their side-table, she stood without speaking and came close to him. She smiled. Their bodies touched without a word. They brought their lips so close that their breaths, with the fragrance of love, magnetically joined together. They kissed lightly and closed their eyes as their lips played the game of love.

Their eyes opened, leaving lips pressed tightly. They took long breaths and then kissed again, and again. They flopped down on the bed and began to undo their clothes. Suddenly, hearing a knocking at the door, they briskly stood, set their clothes in order, and took books in their hands.

Alisha opened the door.

"Hi, Alisha. Where were you?" her two friends asked. "We looked for you in the library and canteen."

"Hi, I'm studying here with Zahid. Come, come. I've told him about both of you."

"Zahid, she is Asima. And he is Azhar. They're a couple who study together."

"Hello," Zahid said. "Nice to meet you, but now I've got to go back to my room. I've some important work to do. Next time, we can work on some Algebra formulas."

"Bye, Alisha," Zahid said and went out of the room.

Shortly after school started, Zahid got a job in a private school in the city of Daren. Within some months, he earned his monthly expenditure and didn't ask his mother for any further money.

Zahid and Alisha studied their honeyed subject of love more than any other subject. They began their love from study in the class, in the canteen, in the library and in the room, in the garden and even on the beaches. Their love story became famous in the university.

When Zahid told Alisha about his mother's simplicity and poverty, Alisha emphatically stated, "I'll not live in the village with you and your mother. My father will give me a beautiful house in the city. There your mother can live with us. I love you, Zahid."

After one year, Zahid smiled and told his mother, "I love the most beautiful girl, Alisha, who belongs to a rich family." Nasreen was happy and wanted to see her. But Zahid didn't answer his mother.

Both wanted to marry during college, but Alisha's parents didn't want this because they thought her studies should come first.

"Do you want to be some old widow living off the sale of the jewelry your husband gave you? Finish school first, my daughter!" her father would say.

Within a few years, Alisha became pregnant before they were married. When Alisha's parents learned about their daughter's condition, she and Zahir were simply and immediately married.

***

"The fingertips were less burnt than the rest of the body, but there was no skin under the nails. There is some defensive bruising on the arms, but the old lady was beaten really hard before she was hit over the head. It wasn't the first beating, either." The coroner said.

Inspector Haider rubbed the back of his neck.

***

Nasreen, unaware of her son's marriage, lived in her house in the hope that one day Zahir would reach the peak of success. Then she would live with him. She'd see him marry his true love, Alisha. See him get a good job, and buy or build a beautiful house in the city. Then she'd leave this village and live a comfortable life.

One day, while sitting in the corridor of her house and looking toward the city, a car stopped before her house. A beautiful girl dressed in lavender silk got out of the car with her son. He jumped up and ran to Zahir. Hugging and kissing him, she said, "I thought about you just now, my son."

"Mother, this is my bride, Alisha," Zahid said. We married one month ago. Now, I've come here to take you to live in our beautiful house. Let's go live in Alisha's home. She is beautiful and kind and loves both you and I."

"How are you, Aunt Nasreen?" Alisha asked, "I'm so glad to meet you. Zahid always praises you. Yes, we want you to live with us. As we go to uni-

versity our house is empty much of the time. Your presence in the house will fill it."

Nasreen wanted to hug her daughter-in-law, but Alisha only shook hands.

Zahid said, "Mother, I've got not a good, but a great job. Now, we live in the city. Leave this village forever!"

"Okay, Zahid. How could you marry and not even tell me? You're my only child, my one son."

"Oh mother! Leave these old dreams. I've talked to a person in the village who will buy this house."

Silently taking some clothes and other things, she followed her son out, and he grandly opened the car door for her. She sat in a car for the first time. It looked so tight and smooth and well made. She left her little house. The car pulled up in front of a grand new house. Her son ushered her up the steps. He took her to look at each room. One was bigger than her whole house. It had gorgeous decor, a dining hall, a television lounge, kitchen and bathrooms. Looking at all the luxurious furniture and the beautiful colors of the house, she rubbed her eyes and said, "Zahid, I'm in paradise. I've never seen its like before."

"Everything is of Alisha's choice. Her parents provided all these things without our asking or demanding anything." Zahir opened a door and led her inside. "Mother, this is your room. What do you want to eat? The kitchen is well stocked; take whatever you like, cook, and eat. We're going out and will come back late tonight. Tomorrow, we'll discuss with you further. Goodbye for now."

***

With the passage of time, the ups and downs of life brought Zahid Malak to squabble with his wife, who took it out on his mother. Alisha always endeavored to create drama in the home, telling her husband, "Your mother has tried to poison my food." Zahid, without knowing whether what his wife had told him was either true or a false, quarreled with his mother even to the point of dragging her out of the house.

Her son, of whom she'd dreamt as a star, to whom she'd looked for support during the last period of her life, now heard only what this wife put in his ears. Overall, Nasreen had a son; no other child nor husband. He was her only hope, but now he had become not only neglectful, but abusive.

One day, after a particularly violent episode, she complained about her son and daughter-in-law at the police station. She had bruises on her arms, but this was an all-too-common domestic matter so far as the police were concerned. The police called Zahid, and after some advice, threatened him with charges if he did not behave better toward his mother,or found a way to control his wife's demeanor.

In this way, he apologized to his mother, before the police. He hugged and respectfully kissed her forehead. His demeanor and apology melted her heart. Taking back her complaint, she went back with him.

***

Alisha noticed her husband's renewed affection toward his mother, and it irritated her. All the strife made life in the household unbearable to the point where one day, without reason or cause, Alisha started to shove her mother-in-law out of the house. Her shoving soon turned to beating, but Zahid put his arms around his mother and sought to pull her away. At that moment, when Nasreen could not fend off a blow because her arms were trapped at her sides, Alisha seized the fireplace poker and struck her twice on the head before Zahid could stop her.

Shortly afterward, Nasreen died. Alisha looked at Zahid, who was crying. She patted his shoulder and hugged him. I'm glad that the old woman is gone for good, she thought. While she held him, she said, "Zahid, we can't call the police; we'll be blamed for having killed her. We should secretly bury or burn her corpse. If we destroy the body, there will be no witness and no evidence."

Alisha pulled the top sheet off his mother's bed and together, they wrapped it around the body. Zahid took the bundle in his arms, which was lighter than he expected, and placed it in the trunk of the car. There was no deserted place in the city, so they drove with no destination in mind.

"You think of something, Alisha. I'm very distraught!"

"Then we should bury it."

"It will take time. If someone sees, then we'll be caught."

"Zahid, listen. There is one quick and effective way to be rid of the body. We should burn it and bury all evidence. No one will be able to identify a burnt corpse, and it'll only take some minutes. Buy petrol. Pour and splash over the corpse. Set it on fire. Run from the spot."

"Yes, it is good. Now, you wait in the car. I'll go buy a few liters of petrol."

"Okay, darling!" Alisha said, kissing him, "Go and get it swiftly. I don't like sitting in the car with a corpse in it."

***

After two days, the burnt and unknown corpse of a woman found in the forest of Musa was reported as breaking news on the different channels and in various papers. The difficult case was being investigated by the famous police officer, Inspector Haider. "It is a murder, since she was killed by a blow to the head, with a small cylindrical object. This is a brutal crime followed by the barbarous act of burning the corpse. One perpetrator wore ladies sandals. We have proof confirming the killers, but we won't show it at this time. In a few days, we'll arrest the authors of this savage crime."

Alisha screamed and called, "Hey, Zahid, come see this!"

Zahid came and looked, and then said, "If anyone asks about mother, say she has gone to her village. We must try to carry on as though everything is normal. It is better for you that you go to your parents for a few days and don't mention this matter. Tell them that we have fought and aren't speaking to each other."

***

Haider sat in his office, talking on the phone with a police officer from another station.

"Do you have any information or records of a complaint of abuse from a woman whose age may be around 43 years old recorded there? Okay, thank you. I'm sorry to trouble you."

Haider put the phone on the table and looked at Sadiq, "What's the matter with you? You look troubled."

"I'm thinking about a matter related to a mother and her son and wife that my grandmother, Javeeriya, mentioned some months ago."

"It's an important thing, Sadiq. What did your grandmother tell you?" Haider asked.

"A poor woman called Nasreen, who lived in our village, complained about her son and daughter-in-law at the police station. I think, sir, that it was the Daren Police Station," Sadiq said, sadly. "Her son's name is Zahid Malak."

Haider jumped up and said, "Sadiq, get up now. First, we'll meet your grandmother, Javeeriya. Later, we'll go to the Daren Police Station. Then we'll visit Zahid Malak, to ask him about his mother, Nasreen."

Haider took his phone from the table. He dialed the number of the S.H.O of the Police Station of Daren and asked him to check the records for any complaints from a woman named Nasreen, six or seven months ago.

Javeeriya told them, "Nasreen had nothing but troubles from her son and his wife, Alisha. So sad, after she helped him with college. That woman was a great mother, but she lived with her son as a servant."

Haider also received a call from Daren Station and heard Nasreen's complaint against her son, Zahid and his wife, Alisha, over the phone.

"I think it best that you send a police officer to examine the situation."

Within three hours, that officer reported. Zahid had said that his mother had gone back to her village to meet her old friend, Javeeriya.

***

Alisha came back to her house after a few days, and Zahid went to his office, as usual. A man called Alisha at home and told her without introduction, "The police have arrested Zahid Malak from his office, for what, I don't know."

Her whole body started shivering, and she cried. Alisha didn't know what to do. She called her par-

ents. They came immediately, and her father went to the police station.

Crying and screaming in her room, Alisha said, "Help me, Mother. I can't bear to go to jail. I hated my mother-in-law so much. We were all yelling, and suddenly, I wanted her gone. I am a murderess."

There was loud banging at the front door. Her mother answered, and the police entered the house. As Alisha lay on the bed, suddenly her hands were pulled behind her.

"Alisha Malak, you're under arrest for the murder and desecration of the corpse of Nasreen Malak."

Zahid Malak had confessed to all crimes. Alisha had always worn golden bangles on her arms, but now they were replaced by handcuffs. She once sat only in luxury cars, now she was a criminal in a police car. She'd always walked with her head up, but now she bowed her head as a judge pronounced her guilty.

Next day, the main headline of a newspaper read:

A MOTHER KILLED AND BURNT

Nasreen, a 43-year-old woman, wife of Waqar Malak, was killed and burnt by her son, Zahid and his wife, Alisha. The corpse was found in Musa's forest and reported to the police. After a week-long investigation by Inspector Haider, mysteries and secrets were laid bare. The deep and silent woods didn't hide the son's & daughter-in-law's barbarism for long.

DRUDGE
Bryan Oliphint

Day #186 of the Repetition. I'm sure of my count. A Right-Foot-Blue Day.

I've started eating whatever came in the mail. Today: flower petals, a bar of chocolate, and some salmon. Fuck it, I'll live.

That's not where I meant to begin. Not at all.

My name. My name is Drudge. Drudge McPherson.

That's me, though I'd rather eat stems and thorns than hear my name one more time. Whether repeated by Jessie or cycled and recycled through my brain. Damned thing's stuck on spin.

The word conjures an image, a similitude of my life—the revolving door of days, each the same as the other, like the blankness of a journal not yet written in, but with the pages numbered and the work considered complete, published, done and finished, with all its white redundancy—the only recurrent entry.

"Hi, my name is Drudge."

If Jessie ever left me, I can just imagine, with horror, the prospect of introducing myself to another living being.

The really hard part about the name though, the really strange part—the detail I've been building up to—the thing I've been disinclined to share, for it unsettles me just to think about it…

I believe I had another name once.

I know that sounds ridiculous. It is ridiculous. But I did have another name. In fact, I think I had more than one. But that was a long time ago—before the Repetition of Days. Before Jessie lost her mind. Before my life became a turnstile without an exit.

I'm trying so hard to sound conversational, but I am shaking. I've had to stop three times because I've reached the point of convulsing.

It's all because of the others.

There, I've said it. They may be watching now. And if they are, I don't know what the consequences will be. If I can just write this out, if I can just believe that someone, somewhere—who isn't one of them—is hearing me, then maybe I will feel better

I won't speak any more of the others. I never know when they are watching. I know that they are watching in the morning. Every morning. (Though it isn't really morning, though Jessie thinks it is, so I call it morning). They are also watching in the evening. I can hear their voices clearly then.

No, I can't speak of them.

I guess I've said all I can about my name. There's nothing else to say, only it bothers me so to discuss it and I don't know why.

My God, I just threw up.

Day #189, a Left-Foot-Blue Day. A pound of almonds, one sleeve of cookies, more chocolate, as usual, a stick of gum (rationing the gum).

"Moooorning Druuuudge!"

She's rocking up on her toes, looking past the sink of dishes, peering over the high window ledge to the crystal-clear view of a brick wall, the next building over, maybe ten feet away. She'd been humming to herself, dancing.

Crazy bitch.

In spite of her happy disconnect from reality, she looks as dismal as my heart. Wretched, really. Barefoot, in her housecoat. Not that any of this hides her curves, mind you. I remember when she used to wear the fanciest of dresses. When people used to stop her on the street just to take pictures. Now this is the only way I see her. Exactly the same. Every day. Every hair, every loose thread.

She makes a half pirouette to face me, feigns a little bow, smiles.

That half-second before the bow; it's the most important part of my day. I am a glanceable mess of mundanity, but you must understand; it's imperative that I get it RIGHT.

Faded red tie, blue slacks—always blue slacks, my one white shirt.

I wore another shirt once, because there was a stain on this one. But she didn't like the new one. I can tell. I can tell in that half-second. She'll raise one eyebrow a little if I fail her. For some reason she liked the old shirt, so I threw the other one away.

I've made other mistakes. Displeased her. I wore the wrong shoes once. Another time I wore a belt. The suit was really made to have a belt and I thought it wouldn't hurt. But that morning she just stared at the belt as if it were some dead thing hanging from my waistline. I threw the belt away. In fact, I threw all my other clothes away. It is best to avoid mistakes.

I said, as I always do, "Stuff it, Jess." I shoved old plates—the same old plates—out of my way and sat down at the table. I hate to speak to her that way. But she insists. I can see it in her eyes. How or when she came to like it, I don't even remember.

Coffee. Newspaper. And then it starts. The Morning Fight. Crazy, noisy voices in my head the whole time, laughing, screaming.

I change the subject. I try to talk about work. I want her to know what I go through so that she can dance ballet from one end of the apartment to the other, pausing to add a few strokes of paint to one of her canvases, singing so loud that the neighbors bang on the wall and bombard her with insults. (She shouldn't shout back, you know).

I am a knight, just like any man, and she just doesn't get it. Without armor, I face my world. I have my dragons to slay. I tell her this.

She stifles a laugh.

"Go ahead..." I mock her posture, her face, her whole insidious delusion. "I'll take my dragon down—and when he crashes to the earth, he'll shatter this city."

I'm talking about my boss, of course. The madman of Manhattan. I've told Jess about him, all the evil that he's done—and how I, the tiny accountant in cubicle number 23, will bring the monster crashing to his knees.

"Oh Drudge... I know you mean it... I really do. But men like that—when they fall..." She wanders off as far as she can in our crappy little apartment. "They fall on people like us, Drudge. And us? We barely make a squeak."

I snatch up my coat. Pick up my briefcase. I turn to find her holding out my lunch. A simple, brown paper bag. I snatch it from her.

And then as I walk across the floor...my shoes... they...

Squeak.

Squeak, squeak, squeak.

I pause to open the door.

"Don't look back," I tell myself.

One more squeak, I'm out the door.

I face the dragon, sword drawn.

By sword, I mean mechanical pencil, freshly loaded with spindly little sticks of graphite.

By facing the dragon, I mean that I am I hunkered down in cubicle 23, a half dozen ledger books spread open. I've done this for the last 189 days. I tell myself that someday it will matter.

But who knows? Maybe this is the day, right? Maybe today it will all end differently.

Clunk. Shuffle, shuffle, shuffle.

Maybe not today. Today—just like every day—a stack of papers has been dropped on my desk by the office mule, who then drags herself off to Cubicle 22. Eager hands reach out, clutching their stash (a much smaller pile than mine) as if it were gold. After the mule is five entryways down, a head pops out of 22.

"Drudge, Drudge, Drudge. Don't be looking at the office mule that way. Everyone knows you have far better at home—even the big boss!"

The head and its pretty face disappear, but then the voice continues. "Hell, Drudge, you have far better right here."

"Uh huh, Marge, you just keep it right there." I hold my hand out as if I were stopping a car. She can't see this motion, of course, but I know she can feel it.

My one friend here. The office whore. She loves me because I won't sleep with her. She also hates me because I won't sleep with her. It's complicated. But still, she's a friend. I like her because I can tell her anything. I also like her because she doesn't understand a damned thing I tell her. If she did comprehend, then she'd repeat it, and if she repeated it, I'd be fired.

"TWENTY-THREE."

The roar of the dragon. He's spotted his prey.

I stand, keenly aware that from across the room, viewed from the madman's high office, my thin frame looks like a startled ostrich rising above a never-ending stand of savannah grass. I can hear the laughter in my head.

"In my office, 9:30 sharp."

I nod. And then I do what I always do; I bury my head in the sand.

Why do the people I love use my name... and the one person I hate calls me by the only thing I can think of that is worse... an impersonal number? He does this to everybody. Except Marge. He calls her honey, as if he's nothing more than a cliché bad boss. But he's not a cliché, is he? I say this because I know more. Much more. Where others see scribbled columns of numbers, I see overcharged rent in hovels that aren't up to the most meager of safety codes. That's always been my gift; to see past the numbers.

The 9:00 break finds me with Marge and two cups of coffee. Both cups are mine. She doesn't drink the stuff, so I joke that I must keep the balance in the world.

I lay it all out. The things I know. The things I see. Hints at what I plan to do.

She smacks her gum. Smiles. She's not from Manhattan. She's from Georgia and I don't know how she ever made it in the big city. Ok, that's not true. I do know. I'm reminded of it as she places her hand on my thigh as she talks, slips it just a bit higher than is appropriate.

"Drudge, listen baby, I sense that you have a problem with what the boss has been doing. Is that what I'm hearing?" Cocks her head.

("Watch out," my mind screams. "Here it comes!")

"I've always been an optimist—a glass-half-full sort of girl. This kind of negativity... well, I don't..."

Blah, blah, BLAH! She yammers on. I've heard it all a hundred times. We've played this out over and over. She's an optimist. Like Jenn, but worse. Hell, Marge busts out in song twice a day.

She's fucking blind.

"Marge," I interrupt, but she continues.

"Marge, you're my friend—but you're a fool."

I feel her hand recoil from my leg.

"You think I'm a pessimist, but I'm not. A pessimist is every bit a fool as an optimist, don't you see? It doesn't matter if the cup is half full or half empty. You know what matters, Marge?"

She blinks like a newborn calf. I'm wasting my words on her, I know, but it doesn't stop me.

"It matters what is IN the cup. And it matters whether or not you have the guts to drink it. Before each one of us sits a cup."

I shove what ought to be her cup of coffee in front of her. I grab my own and peer into it as if I were gazing into a crystal ball.

"It's the stuff of our lives. And it does not matter if the cup is half full or half empty. That is a fool's question."

"Oh, I suppose that in some dark hour we may feel better if we decide that the cup is half full—that the more problems and trials and decisions we face, the more it is reflective that we have a full life and that we have the opportunity to live life fully. But the real question, the important question, is whether or not we are willing to drink the cup. No matter how bitter a brew is drawn for us, it is our privilege alone to taste of it."

"We must drink up the draught of life, savor its mingled flavors, though salty like sweat, or sweet like pressed fruit, sometimes fermented, sometimes fresh, one swallow hot, another bitter cold, the next one warming us like underclothes fresh out of a dryer on a cold winter day.

"Let's drink now and again we will drink tomorrow, and we'll drink every day until we see the bottom of the cup."

"Let's drink."

She looks from the cup and back to me at least three times.

"But Drudge," she says, "you know I don't like coffee."

Echoing down the hall, I hear a voice, "Hey twenty-three!"

An even 200, a Right-Foot-Blue Day. Or it was one.

Did I do anything different with the boss that day? Or any day since? What did I think I was going to do? He's smarter than me. Sure, I have a gift for seeing the problems; but he has the brains to have created the whole thing—and the brilliance to get away with it, to navigate the complex sea of lies far beyond the simple shores of my stupid little cubicle. To take him down would take down politicians, police officers without a moral code, and God knows who else. My speeches and my posturing are all for nothing. I spread my peacock feathers in front of Jessie and Marge—and then when I'm dragged into the high office, what do I do? I let him browbeat me. I make jokes at his expense, sure, and he doesn't catch them—not because he's stupid, but because he lacks a sense of humor. And while that feels good, it does nothing at all to solve the problem.

My boss isn't the real enemy anyway. I said I wouldn't speak of them, but things have happened.

In the kitchen, after my half-second inspection, I opened my paper, expecting to find the same tired articles that are always there.

A piece of paper hung taped between the pages. A few words of Jessie's handwriting. Even before I read it, I could see how smooth her script was—as curvy and flowing and beautiful as ever.

They have gotten to her fully now.

Her handwriting is not like mine. It is not the script of someone who has fought them off for so long. It is the script of someone who is happy in their world. Perhaps my writing will become more like hers and stop going all over the page like this little journal of mine does. Her note was simple enough—and the words that were written there caused my heart to pound loudly in my chest until I could hear the blood rushing in my ears.

"They love it, hon. We won!"

THEY love it.

I looked up at Jessica from my paper, her hair flopped this way and that, her robe wrapped frumpily against her body, disguising its true form.

She's lost to me and she will never return.

It was time to go on with my day. I stumbled through it all a freshly broken man.

On the way home, I encountered a most unusual person; he was dressed like me. When I say, "dressed like me," I mean that he was dressed exactly like me—same blue jacket, same red tie, same white shirt. My God, the shirt—the stain—there was a stain on the shirt exactly where my stain is!

There was one thing wrong though…the socks. The socks, damn it.

I have one blue sock, one black one, you see? I swap them each day, left and right, and Jessie never notices. It's been my private little rebellion, the one thing I do to push back against them.

I wash them each night in the sink, drape them across the side to dry. And then—and only just right then—do I put a hashmark on the inside of the cabinet. And then—and only just right then—do I reverse the socks.

Maybe it's not that important, swapping those socks—it's the only thing keeping one day from blending into the next, the only thing keeping me from going down Jessie's path to madness.

This man—the other me. What is the meaning of it all? He walked right up, then assumed my stance. I stepped back; he stepped back. I started to call out; he opened his mouth.

Wait.

It occurs to me now—now that I am writing this. His briefcase—I held mine in my right hand. He held his in his left. The socks—the briefcase—his motions.

He was my mirror image.

Suddenly he stood at attention like a soldier. Smiled, eyes dancing. Bowed (like Jessie bows each morning). And set his briefcase down in front of me.

Then he turned and walked away. I wish now that I had seen where he went, but my eyes were locked on the briefcase. I stood there quite a while, unsure what to do. I decided there was nothing else I could do except pick it up and take it with me.

I've sat with it here for what seems eternity. There's nothing left to do but open it.

I washed my socks a bit ago, slowly, carefully, afraid of the decision I had to make. I stood there with them wadded up in my hands. I just didn't know, still don't know, what the meaning of the man was—and whether I could continue my rebellion— whether I could mark my day and—oh God—I don't know if I can—if I can just one more time— or ever again—swap the socks.

How can such a simple thing become the most important thing in the world?

They're crumpled up in the sink now and I'm sitting here with the briefcase.

I'm laughing now. I wish you could have seen this—whoever the hell you are reading my journal. I've sat here this whole damned time trying to find the courage to open the briefcase—I've cried, I've fretted, I've paced back and forth, even rinsed the socks out again. And when I finally open the case, it's the wrong damned one!

I'd swapped the cases somewhere along the way, maybe when I set them down to unlock the door? So I open the case and in it are two ledgers, a stack of papers, etcetera. My stuff. At first, I panicked. I thought, "Oh my God, even THIS is the same." But then I grabbed the other case and flung it open. Didn't even have time to think about it.

The case contains a sort of oversized coin on a stand. On the coin are two faces: one happy, the other sad, and a name I don't recognize.

I guess that I'm the happy face right now. It's been so long since I laughed.

But I'm not just laughing at what happened with the cases; I've had an idea. The cases are identical. I've looked them over thoroughly. Except my case is scuffed on the bottom!

I've set my socks out. Right one's blue, just like today. No swapping socks now, no swapping them tomorrow, no swapping ever again. I've made a fresh hashmark inside the cabinet door. I set the stand holding the oversized coin inside the cabinet and shut the door. I swapped my ledgers and papers over to the other briefcase.

And so now on the table sits the case, ready for work tomorrow.

Tomorrow.

Tomorrow: Day 201, a No-Scuff Briefcase Day. The rebellion continues.

Day 204, a Scuffed Briefcase Day.

Somebody signed me up for the Fruit-of-the-Month Club. It's a sad, sad day when the most beautiful thing you've laid eyes on in a long, long time is a box of fuzzy brown fruit.

Kiwis weren't all that came in the mail. I received a big, puffy envelope, the sort that you normally send documents in that you don't want to fold, except this was stuffed with something soft and lumpy. Normally I pass on such packages. I get so many, you know, and from God knows where and for God knows why, and if I can tell they don't contain food, I just pile them in what used to be a closet. The closet is stuffed from floor to ceiling now and I can't close the door, so maybe that's part of why I opened the package.

And I laughed again. Twice in one day, third time in a week—like that's a record, you know, at least since the Repetition began. I teased open the corner and saw a bit of yellow cloth, tore the paper down the seam and dumped it out. I didn't even know they made such things.

Happy little smiley faces all over a pair of yellow boxer briefs.

Another arrow in the quiver of my little rebellion. I put on the underwear. In fact, I took off everything else, rolled my desk chair over to the dining room table where I was opening mail, and spun around a few times.

And then I opened a little box that is destined to change my life. It was small, the sort of box that normally contains jewelry. I didn't know what to expect.

A bullet.

A single, wonderful, beautiful bullet. More gorgeous than kiwis. More gorgeous than me in my boxer briefs!

I stayed up all night thinking how to make this work. In the morning, two hours before sunrise, it came to me. I dismantled my desk chair and two lamps before I found a piece of metal tubing the right diameter. The chair also yielded a welcome surprise; it contained a bearing. Twenty minutes of smacking it against a brick wall and out spilled a pile of greasy little metal balls, a little bigger than BB's. An antique clock became the next victim and I had a serviceable spring and a pile of other potential parts.

Fifteen minutes before it was time for coffee with Jessie, I had something that might work. I'll keep tinkering, but it won't be long.

I'll have something that can fire a bullet.

Day 209, a No-Scuff Briefcase Day

The dashes and the dots, the links between the things that matter and the things that had not (until now) been worth a second thought. My God, I should have seen it.

Sorry, I'm not making sense.

It's like a puzzle, all the pieces poured from the box, a jumble. Sure, I'd found the corners, assembled some of the sides. I thought I saw the picture. I was wrong.

The pieces, so random: My apartment. Crappy, but the best one in the building. Spencore—the Madman's company, entered over and over in the ledger books. Being called every day to his office. The urgent assignment that always has me working through lunch. The rent checks being payable to Spendthrift Properties.

Are you not seeing it?

It's ok; I didn't see it either. Not for all these never-ending days, I didn't see it. And when I did see it, I didn't believe it. But even Marge knew. Bitch didn't tell me! Or maybe she tried to. What was it she always says? "Everyone knows you have far better at home—even the big boss!"

I skipped my assignment today, crept back to the apartment door, leaned against it, and there I found the truth.

Here, I'll help you if you're not getting it: the Madman is fucking Jessie.

There you go.

And I'm sitting here, shoved up in the corner, cradling my one-shot answer, trying to decide.

Decide. Decide. Decide.
Where to waste my gorgeous bullet.
I hate her. I hate him. I hate them.
I hate me.
Decide. Decide. Decide.

Excerpt from a press release, Saturday, October 13, 11:30 p.m. EST, New York City:

Tony Award-winning actor Nicholas Samuelson shot himself dead before a live audience at 8:27 p.m. EST. Famously eccentric, Samuelson was known for "falling into" his rolls, staying in character even off set, for as long as the show ran on Broadway. After taking a six-year break from the stage, Samuelson resurrected his career with his latest and last roll as Drudge McPherson, the half-crazed husband to Jessica McPherson (Samantha Allred) and low-paid underling to Jonathan Spencer (Gene Moncreef) in the award-winning masterpiece, Sheer Drudgery. Even as the play rose to number one in New York and Samuelson's performance earned him this year's Tony Award for Best Actor, Samuelson refused to grant interviews or even speak to anyone other than cast members.

Transcript from the New York News Show, 6 months later:

Candice Winesteen, New York News: You've been quoted as saying that you took this part solely for the purpose of working with Mr. Samuelson.

Gene Moncreef (Jonathan Spencer, aka, the Madman of Manhattan): Yes, I did. Nobody in the business thought this play would make it to production. I had passed on the role already—until it was announced that Nicholas had signed on. I had to swallow my pride and call them back.

Candice: And then it became number #1

Gene: Best decision I ever made.

<laughter>

Candice: Nicholas Samuelson had some committed fans

Gene: Committed is hardly the word for it. He had a following. At least a third of the audience on any given night were regulars—some came once a month, others once a week. They followed his every action. I think it's why he moved into his dressing room at the start of the play.

Candice: Now for some hard questions.

Gene: I'm ready…I think.

Candice: You were on stage that day—the day it happened. Can you talk about it?

Gene: It's not easy, but yes. You know, Nick was famous for rewriting—some called it ad libbing—but it was more than that. He would tweak the plot. The changes would stick and become part of the play. Of course, nobody else could get away with that. But Nicholas—he'd built a career of it. All of us had to be ready to respond on the spot, in the moment, to anything he might say. So when he showed up that day—in a scene he wasn't even supposed to be a part of—I thought Nicholas was taking it to a whole new level.

Candice: But this wasn't a rewrite, was it?

Gene: Well, in a way it was. Some people might be angry at me for saying this, but Sheer Drudgery was a modern-day tragedy that lacked a truly tragic ending. It was the story of one man against the system—who was then destroyed by the system. "Cubicle 23" has become a rally cry for those who are protesting the power of the 1%. In the play, I have an affair with his wife—and Drudge never finds out. By walking into that scene, Drudge changed the play—his character found out the truth.

Candice: So you're saying that Nicholas Samuelson took his own life to give the play a better ending?

Gene: I'm not sure I'm saying that. One thing I am sure of: we will never know.

Candice: This might be a good time to discuss two other things. First, the autopsy.

Gene: Yes, the brain tumor. Nick had a brain tumor the size of an egg.

Candice: Some have suggested that this is why he took his own life.

Gene: I don't believe that. Candice, I've hired two private investigators and also worked alongside the police officers involved in the case, and here's what we've learned; there's no evidence that he ever knew.

Candice: Do you believe it affected him?

Gene: One doctor told me that Nick shouldn't have been able to perform—that he shouldn't have been able to remember his lines.

Candice: The second thing we need to discuss: the journal. You are one of the few who have read it. What can you tell us?

\<long pause>

Gene: I'm sorry. I thought I was ready for this. \<wipes away tears, smiles>

Candice: Take your time.

Gene: The journal. Wow. First let me say, that portions of the journal will be published in January. The proceeds will go to a mix of organizations which combat suicide.

\<applause>

Gene: There's something else I want to say, and this is to those who loved Nick—whether family, or friends, or fans. Before you read this journal, you need to know that Nicholas was—how do I say this? Not himself.

Candice: It's been reported that the journal is written from the perspective of the character. Is this what you mean? Or do you mean something more?

Gene: More. Something much more. That's all I'm going to say on the matter.

Candice: That day—on the stage—after the shot was fired, Mr. Samuelson fell to the floor. I'm sorry, I know this is difficult.

Gene: We didn't think it was real. We thought it was stage blood, but I went to him anyway. That's when I realized that it was real. Very, very real.

Candice: You knelt down beside him. As I am sure you are aware, footage of the incident has recently surfaced. Mr. Moncreef, it appears that Mr. Samuelson said something to you in those last moments.

\<long pause>

Gene: I had told myself I wasn't going to answer any question regarding that. I meant to have my agent convey my wishes. But here we are.

Candice: \<quietly> Here we are.

Gene: \<reluctantly> He said two words: "Wrong decision."

Candice: He regretted killing himself?

Gene: Prior to Drudgery, Nicholas took six years off from acting. During that time, he organized protests against the financial establishment. I believe he regretted, in a way, not finishing what he started, not putting an end to what I represented in the play.

Candice: I'm not sure I understand.

Gene: I have reason to believe—and I blame the tumor for this—that he regretted not shooting me instead.

Elf Amber
M.T. Finnberg

Returning my katanas into the harness on my back, I grab hold of the boulder, kick my boots against the granite, and push my tattooed torso on top. I need to see what's been making the jungle rustle. If it's what I think it is, I've earned this month's salary.

I can already smell this thing. It's close.

I'm not worried. Esposito didn't hire me for being the world's greatest berry picker. Esposito called me because I'm the best specialty hunter this side of society. At least, I like to think that's not off by much.

For the heck of it, I turn my face to the sky and sniff. It makes me gag and cough. The stench is so strong I couldn't dismiss it if I tried.

Now where is this sneaky critter—ah hah! Crouching in the greenery. Not much taller than a four-year old child, but ashen-blue and furry, this elf's hiding in the patch of sturdy agave. I can see his lanky arm twitching between the leaves. He's jittery. Well, he ought to be.

And boy, he smells. Elves reek of rotten cilantro. Some people say the smell reminds you of hand sanitizer—people say that. And yeah, I agree, to an extent, but it's kind of like the foulest-rotten stench of clean you can think of.

I lift my gun. As always, I try not to think about stuff too much. Zzzzap! The sedative dart is stuck in the elf's flank. Shrieking, he bounces up and starts limping off. Disappears into the underbrush.

Ain't no problem, he ain't getting far. I can take it easy now, follow his tracks.

There are days when I hate this job. But gotta play by the rules of the game if you want to eat.

I considered myself a tough goon when I first got to this galaxy sector, but I shed some illusions soon enough. Guys like me get the worst of it. For instance, take the ride I arrived in on this planet, this morning. The Alliance Treasury Secretary's private yacht turned prisoner tow-ship. Dig this: they put two guards on board. Three ex-cons who'd done

time at Nova Siberia—yours truly included—and two guards.

Ok, we were in cryo-chambers under light sleep. But have you seen the typical routine of an inmate at Nova Siberia? Guys there have angel sand for breakfast and a cocktail of downers for dinner. Regular sedatives ain't gonna keep guys like us under. You need to shoot something tougher up our veins, and lots of it, like, what you'd use to take an elephant down: know what I mean?

We're used to stuff. It don't affect us.

So how did the officers not expect to have an empty cryo locker when we reached the planet? I'm guessing they didn't. I'm guessing it was their specific job to lose a few high security charges in the wilderness.

Esposito did give me a job to do once I was planetside, so I guess he trusted I'd be getting out. Suffice it to say, me and the other two goons did so within ten minutes of reaching safe altitude. My script was clean and short: I pulled a stun gun on one of the pilots and had the guy release the doors. Scared him good, but luckily it didn't take much, 'cause honestly, I don't like inflicting pain—sue me. Then I grabbed a parachute, kicked open an airlock, and dove out like a frigging swan.

Free fall. Ten minutes of the sweetest damn freedom I've ever tasted. I was a bird in the sky, I was fireworks.

Short party. I landed in a snake fang tree, which I figure was extra venomous. The stinging rash left me looking like I'd suddenly caught smallpox, like some mutant kind of smallpox, like bad, even though I took the all-around antidote pills that guys like me kind of have to carry.

Thanks to my mercenary training, I finally know my way around survival skills. I say finally, 'cause I waited fifteen years for that. As a kid back in the dusty suburb alleys of North LA, ever since my stepdad kicked me around I dreamt of the army. That's what my Shangri La looked like: get okayed for the army, get a military training, learn to keep myself safe.

They didn't take me in the Alliance army, because I had a history of petty thefts. That sucked, because I'd already done time for it. Besides it was just groceries and some electronics that I put to better use. Heck, I got old Mrs. Hansen a wrist pad, so she could call her grandkids when she got in trouble. That's what I'd stolen, that and some random home appliances.

Those corners, you gotta do what you can to get by, you know what I mean? If you ask me, I'm not a bad guy. Wouldn't want to swat a fly. I'm the irritating guy who'll complain about people letting their cats out in the streets at night in L.A., where the communal maintenance bots will get them—if the stray dogs don't eat them—'cause I don't stomach that kind of thing well.

One big mistake I do admit to. I stole a hovercraft once and pocketed some stuff I thought nobody would miss. Only, it turned out, some peeps were hiking and got into trouble since they'd had no ride home. That sucked. I wasn't happy. What can I say? My apologies, man.

Photo by Mimi Garcia on Unsplash

Anyway, I think the Alliance should have drafted me, but okay, they get to take their pick.

Luna Mercenary Core was happy to have me, and the feeling was mutual. It was like coming home to the home I never knew.

The Core gives you a gun, teaches you how to use it, teaches you how to defend yourself, and that's what I'd needed, always had. So I got my long-craved fair share of yelling by a sarge, and I was on cloud nine.

And then I was out in the world, with this training, with this gun, and it turned out that the best clients, showing up to hire Luna trained mercenaries, were outer star system mafia. See what I mean? Gotta do what you gotta do.

Fast forward to me here, on some planet I don't actually know the name of, on a mission to meddle in some local mining business dispute. An elf amber mine.

Yeah, Esposito planted me on that prisoner transfer trusting I'd get out soon enough. I'm on a need-to-know basis—so much so that I don't know what the heck I'm doing—but I do know I need to hunt me an elf and get him to do some flying.

Esposito supplied me with fancy gear, even the kind you can hide on your body—the kind that fools the medical systems—unless somebody actually downloads the chip's data to look at it. Esposito had his surgeon put a few chips in me that look like regular chips, but they've got magic, so now I can create a surge of psi power. They say it's a neuro-affector and not real magic, but I ain't buying that. Nah, it's magic, and I feel like an angel of wrath.

No? I think I pass nicely for an angel of wrath. I've already shot down from the skies, and now I'm wading in what looks like a primordial jungle, stung by a snake fang tree. I'm sure between my grimace and my rash, I look pretty wrathy. Is that a word? It's a word. Yeah.

Esposito knew who he was hiring.

The thing is, I know all about creatures of any value from here to Nova Siberia, because that's how I used to escape the world. Books and media were my way out. I didn't have to survive the alleys playing punch bag to bullies if I sat home watching vids about other worlds. So I became the unofficial professor of what's-its-name-critters-of-strange-worlds. I know how they tick. What they eat. Where they hide. What they do when they attack.

I knew becoming a specialty hunter would be my ticket out of that life. The only thing was, reading in the light of my phone, hunched down in my grimy room, I didn't know how to use a gun or a net or anything much, and this thought kept pestering me: how do I make this real? I knew what I had to do: learn to stand up for myself, then learn some combat skills. Not even just for critter hunting, but for survival. I couldn't get that thought out of my head. That's why Luna Core was my heaven.

After Luna, I will now jump on an oolaflump single-handed, no problem whatsoever. Luna was no play park.

Without thinking, I've wrangled the elf down and tied its legs and arms. I get these blackouts sometimes. I go absent, don't know what I'm doing. I guess I'm just too immersed in my own world, in the flow, you know? Ain't no harm in that, is there? Or is there?

Anyway, I don't have to concentrate too much on taking down a four-foot elf, never mind the nine-foot wings with them poison claws; this ain't the first elf I've caught. I've been hired to hunt elves before. They're one of the common items. I don't know what people do with them. Needed for the work-force, I guess. I don't tend to ask questions. I wish I could ask, but I can't.

Once in a grocery store on Cava Waga, I saw a shelf stacked with insect repellent that was suppos-edly made with elf sweat—that's what the etiquettes said. Who knows what really went into those bot-tles? Does one want to know? But people do hunt these critters, for whatever purpose. So, could have been elf sweat, not saying it couldn't. And I know there's a brand of pesticide that advertises 'natural elf oil', too, nine percent. I've seen these products around. Heck, nine percent, like you might not want to buy this stuff if there was any less? Yeah. Nice, nice… a lot goes on around this corner of the world that I really don't want to know too much about.

And it's not like I haven't seen my share. I've been around. Nova Siberia, high security detention center: I served time—three years. Followed by with the sweet Luna Army Base: my military training—two years.

So, I've been around, but this galaxy sector is something else.

I've always secretly wished the Alliance militia would rocket over, raid this neighbourhood, and put an end to all the hazy business. It's sad, it really is.

I fling the elf on the self-inflating sledge from my supplies and cover its bewildered face with a sack.

Could have carried the poor bastard, but I would have choked halfway to our destination with the stench. No offense. They can't help it.

After a three-hour hike, I recognise the high-rise building from the brief: The Aldebaran Con-vention center. This glass-walled skyscraper is the only building around for miles, standing alone in a stretch of desert land. Main function: to act as a physical address for bank transfers and business deals that require considerable slack in the paper-work.

I get out the tablet Esposito gave me. It's the most expensive man-made artifact I've held in my hands. I believe it costs more than, say, the L.A. block house my apartment was in.

When I turn on the holo projector, blue lights spring up to dance above the gadget's mirror sur-face. A gurgling sound belts out words in the crude language of the elves, and it's like the voice is cack-ling.

But the elf seems to catch on. Its nose is twitch-ing. Apprehensive?

"Me fly up-up? Find button?"

"You know English?"

"Me work at mine, know little."

"Okay… so you got that? Fly up and take down the surveillance systems. The cameras don't care about you elves. I guess there's so many of you flapping around all the time, and normally you're no harm."

"You let me goo, me fly, get it, get it, get it!"

"Do I get what? Oh, you'll get the job done? If I let you fly, you'll do as the instructions say? Prom-ise?"

"Yes, yes, yes! Proomis!"

"Do you even know what a surveillance system is?"

"No, no, no. Tell Gubba, then Gubba know. Gubba good eyes and ears."

"Heck, just follow the instructions."

I hear people walking toward us, still out of sight behind the corner, talking in casual voices. I press a hand over the elf's mouth and make the cut-throat gesture, drawing a line across my throat. The critter looks like he understands. See what my job's like? I hate this. Tell me what else a guy's to do.

This is what happens when all the big money's in the hands of—let me cite a favorite song—people hard of heart. Don't be surprised; I listen to music. I ain't learned, but I ain't completely uneducated either. Anyway, some people might say the suits leading the Syndicate are real-life sociopaths. I ain't one to say that, I try to stay in terms. So let's say a little hard of heart.

I wave toward the bushes, and the elf scrambles into the foliage of the hibiscus fence that lines the walkway between me and the glass wall.

The second he's out of sight, a group of men emerges from behind the corner. Their faces react in a dozen different ways as they spot me.

"Who the hell is this guy?" A middle-aged man in front, wearing glasses, literally stiffens up as he apparently comes to the conclusion that I'm up to no good. "People, I think we've got a trespasser. Hey, you! What do you think you're doing? Got some spray cans in there? Protester? Got something against elf amber mining, huh?"

I try to think fast to come up with a good story. Why didn't I think of this beforehand? Esposito didn't prepare me for this.

"I'm talking to you. You with them protesters?"

"Maybe," I grunt like an idiot. I don't really know where I stand, because I don't know Esposito's plans. I only have my orders. Guys like me are cannon fodder.

"Well, we've got permits. I don't have time for this."

I want to laugh out loud, but I don't. Not with his eyes like that. But I know it's illegal to mine wild elf amber. You can cultivate it under government-issued licence, but you sure as hell can't go to natural elf habitats and start digging up their amber. Elves make it from the sap of a tree that grows all over the Aldebaran A sector—a gnarly tree with blue bark that can live up to five hundred years. Can't remember the name of it, though I suppose I should. In practice, it seals the elves' death sentence, because they're being driven out of their habitats. People oppose that—I know I do—but, what can you do?

The elves are no geniuses. They will tear off branches and poke holes in tree trunks with rocks, then set anything underneath that can trap some sap, such as rocks with dents, or sea shells, or crude 'dishes' wrapped out of large leaves. Then they'll carry the sap, galloping on three limbs, to a spot that they've mutually decided looks good. When they have enough sap, they dig up the acidous helian crystal sand and sprinkle it all over, then cover up the whole thing.

The amber is left to 'simmer'. If you dig it up in a few months, the sap has mingled with the ochre crystal sand into a compound known as elf amber. Highly potent stuff for many medical uses, and when used in excess, a psychedelic. Highly sought after.

"Okay, son, why don't you spare us your speech and just file a complaint on me? Senior Field Supervisor Mulholland, with two L's in the middle."

The younger man beside him, with frizzy hair sticking out all over the place, gives Mulholland a concerned look. Mulholland makes a face back at him.

"Does this guy look like he can afford to sue us? He's a cockroach. As long as he doesn't spray the walls…" Mulholland turns back to me. "People like you don't know how this world works. You're crying over the elves not getting their shiny trinkets? Look, the average IQ of one of those stinkers ain't much higher than a chicken. Think they even know what to do with this stuff?" Mulholland lifts a hand in front of his face like ogling at a nugget of amber. "Ooh, prettyyy…I don't know what the heck it is, but it's so prettyyy…"

"They have to eat," a sullen old guy in mechanics' overalls puts in from the back of the group. People turn.

"You got something to say, Grandpa?"

"Yeah. You know the elves eat it. And you might want to know, they actually need it to keep their blood running. Take away their amber, their blood turns brittle. Then I guess you won't be seeing them flying much for you soon, either. You need elf workers. If you don't care about anything else, you might want to think about that. Have you seen them out there in the shrubs? The poor bastards look famished."

"I've seen a few," Mulholland says, jaw tense. "Didn't look that famished to me. One of those suckers tried to bite my arm off. Almost got through my suit. Tech suit, mind you… I was hunting. Frigging monster… Wasn't anything weak about that bite, all I'll say. Heck, if they get any stronger eating amber, then let's not feed them too much amber! Right, ya guys?"

Seeing everyone's faces, Mulholland raises his hands placatingly.

"What? I don't know, I'm just here to do my job, take my pay, then I'm off. I don't need to know if they munch on amber for high tea. Not my concern." Mulholland shoots a murdering glance in my direction. "And you, we don't need no pampered goody-two-shoes over here. You got all of them tattoos, too, think you're so tough? Try living this life, mining business, you ain't gonna last a week. Now, scoot off, get off my premises! I supervise the work around here, I need to make sure my men can work. Get out of my face now and I won't call the guards."

Mulholland frowns at Grandpa. "Don't you get all mushy on me, too. You getting on board with Cool Tattoos here? If you don't like it here, pack up, I ain't stopping you."

The old man looks away, shaking his head.

I watch the elf shivering, curled up in a ball, as the men leave and vanish behind the corner. Apparently I didn't come off as much of a threat, then. They must have thought they talked me out of whatever crazy vandalising stuff I might have been planning. Well, thank you, protesters…

I kneel down and call the elf out.

"Me go now? Go up-up, fly?" He's biting his skinny blue fingers, he looks like he wants to get out of here on any excuse. I don't blame him. I unwrap the rope around his wings, and he opens them up with a gust of stench that has me grabbing my nose.

He's off.

The veined, bat-like leather wings are see-through. The sun catches them, making them glow red. He looks like a broken kite rising in the air

currents along the building's walls.

He reaches the roof-top. A minute goes by. Another. Then I see the yellow LED lights by the side of the door flicker in a sequence and turn green.

Well, color me surprised. He's done it.

I grab my gun and I'm in.

There's nobody in the stairway. I know where to go: doesn't take brains to figure out how to get to the penthouse. I pass seven floors without hearing a thing except my increasingly loud panting. Fifteen. Sixteen. What the heck…? You'd expect guards closing in on me by now. Is this a set-up? Is somebody waiting for me up there?

My hands cramp over the gun handle as I enter the penthouse lobby. Only three steps in I twirl around, heart beating in my ears. I try to advance, but take 360 after 360. Where is everyone? What is this?

The door to the vault is wide open. I was supposed to break that door in if I had to. No need now.

Ready, steady, go. I dive in, gun first.

A fraction of a second is all I have to take in the uniformed guards fleeing the room. They fall and take cover alongside the corridor, pressing themselves into nooks along the walls and behind whatever shelter is available.

There's something behind my back. I have a bad feeling about this.

The second I turn, I question the gods if I'm still alive. Behind me is a plasma gun aimed right past me. I should be dead, but I'm not, because the plasma's not meant for me.

I know the woman who holds that gun. Better than I should. Better than I want to. That's Ellis. Tall, strawberry blonde, and surreally curvy for someone so skinny—and with her amber eyes emboldened with war paint—she looks like a game-play avatar from a corny splatter. When you know her as well as I do, you treat her with certain respect. Otherwise she'll slice you with her katana blades within a second.

She had a reputation at Luna. Guys fell for her left and right, until they snapped out of it and started taking revenge. She made a lot of enemies.

For some reason, I was spared that drama. Maybe because I never thought of her that way—not romantic, anyway. Kept a safe emotional distance. But god, I loved her company. Pitch black humor. The dirtiest jokes. Pranking the commanding officer and squirming out of trouble. In my book: fun.

I don't have an explanation, but we managed to steal one night together without turning into enemies. On watch at the Argon mountains on Gerris 54. Basic army training: no sleep, mindless chores. Bores you to tears. People do stupid stuff, like leave a watch post on watch. We were interrupted, the whole thing was swept under the rug, and we picked up where we left off, as friends, of sorts. Needless to say, easier for her than me.

Honestly, I could never figure out if she gave a second thought over us never taking a step in that direction again. It was kind of a silent agreement. On my part, very quiet, so as not to get a pair of katanas in my back.

Now Ellis has that look in her anime eyes: she has a plan and lets me freely pick my side. She doesn't believe in good people, she believes in "all the right things". I know from her face she's hoping for me to be complicit in some epic crime, no questions asked. This is a Right Thing.

From her gesturing, I get that we need to reach the other side of the room, to get to the computers there. I see, we need to take down the shields and the default security protocols?

"Heck, I don't know the plan, Els. I have a script, I don't know what we're after."

That lights her up into that billion watt smile. She knows I'm going to play along. All I need is directions.

This is why we stayed friends. We share this crazy side. We love us some fun, and underneath it all, we only want that because this world's a sick place and that sucks. You can get killed any day. Better do it for a good cause, right? Ellis thinks so. She and me both.

She knows I'll take a leap for the heck of it. Back when I left L.A. I leapt into the unknown—something worse than I thought I could bear—and

it paid off. I crave that again. Always do.

She takes a few steps towards me. The guards are still waiting for us to make that mistake and try our luck at charging in.

"Let me fill you in. Down in the conference room are a dozen of the greediest, nastiest people in the universe. President of Aldebaran Ore Inc., the CEOs of two of the biggest corporations around this sector, the Terran Finance consul… they're making laws to ensure their corporations can legally take over planets from elves to use for profit." Ellis's eyes burn. "Remember the secondary rights law? That won't be in the way anymore. They're getting rid of it. They don't want human rights for all these creatures. It makes things too inconvenient for them."

I didn't know any of this. I had a tiny part in the play. Ellis had hers. Together, here we are. I feel like a grain of sand on a beach.

"What they don't know is that somebody cracked the code on their correspondence and found out they'd be having their party here. Esposito wants us to hijack this place and give them his terms. I say we do something better. I say we blow this place up."

I notice the gadget Ellis fiddles with in her right hand. "So… I'm guessing we need to download info from the computers and detonate this bomb?" Ellis isn't kidding. She wants to blow up the building. Hold on a second.

"Didn't you get a chip planted?" Ellis says, fussing with putting away her gun and biting her lip as she rests her back to the wall, inches away from starting off those guns on the other side. "Can't you freeze the guards?"

The PSI chip. Yes. It's so new, and so different from anything I'm used to, with my brain fog I didn't even think of it in the middle of all this. I'm used to hit jobs with next to no info—none of these big players want anyone to know anything—but this is on a different level altogether.

I close my eyes, focus like I'm a stone, and power up the PSI.

These guards have probably never seen this

done. This magic costs big money.

I can feel the guards' minds in the distance like gray entities in black mist. I grope around, trying to find my way. I see better with my eyes squeezed closed. Then I put a clamp on all these minds.

"I think I've got them…Wait, Els, just a sec." Can I trust this? It's a gut feeling. I don't know I'm good, it just feels like it.

"Now?" Ellis gives me a deer-like look.

"I don't think it's getting better. This is what I've got. You decide."

"Can you feel them, sort of like you're pressing them down like taffy… kind of?"

"Kind of, yeah. Something like… exactly like that."

"I'm going in. Tell me when."

I focus on the meditation so hard you could put me in a monastery. Ellis dives in. She's through the room. She's at the controls. Downloads stuff onto a memory stick. With a clink, the bomb is secured to the target. She primes it, and a plastic button lights up.

If she presses that button we'll take down some monsters, right? End a dynasty of exploitation?

Ellis reaches out. Her delicate hand stops mid-air—short manicured nails glimmering under the cold, office-type lighting—and hovers above the button like judge and jury. Her eyes are asking me, should I? Should we? And they're saying, we have to do this, somebody's got to do this, it's about time.

I don't always have the luxury of opinion, so much of the time, I don't stop to think. But here, I agree, more than I've agreed with anything in a while. I want to vote on behalf of all the life us humankind are wiping out, as we colonise the stars. On behalf of all the critters I've read about, hiding in my basement room in the haziest corner of North L.A. wearing either of my two sweaters, I want to say, hell, yes. It's about time somebody stood up for the side that's got no voice.

Ellis presses the button.

That's my girl.

I close my eyes waiting for the pressure wave to take me out. Ellis's soft voice yanks me out of it.

"Let's start moving, buddy! We have four minutes to get to the flier up on the roof." Ellis says that like telling me her dog has died. I don't know what to say. I follow. I clamp the guards for two floors, then I can't reach them anymore.

We're hovering above the hazy blue roundness of this deceivingly pristine-looking planet I still don't know the name of, when the explosion shakes the ground.

"Els…I hope your flier can take us somewhere the Syndicate won't be coming after us. Just saying."

"I was thinking, sector H?"

"How are we going to get to sector H? Point zero two light years away?"

"I know somebody's headed there with a freight carrier. An old friend. A smuggler."

"Ah."

"Got better ideas?"

Her stare makes me shake my head. "Me? Guys like me can't afford ideas. I wish we could…"

The Flight
Abigail Wild

My feet burn, there's a cramp in my shoulder, my back hurts, they are all standing too close to me, too close to each other. I'm completely sandwiched between two large Indian families with a bunch of kids running around. One keeps knocking into me. It all feels so… uneasy.

Padati… think about Padati.

He should be waking up for the day. I wonder if he's getting ready for me. There, the butterflies, focus on those! I can't believe I'm taking control of my life. It's about time. Excitement, yes, this is exactly what I need, excitement. Anyone would agree, I'm sure.

A toddler with snot all over his face watches me. I smile and wave at him, he points at me then turns towards his mother who scoops him up. My feet hurt. The line moves forward a bit.

I study the arrival and departure board for what feels like an eternity. My flight departs in three hours, an extremely long time to be alone with my thoughts. My snotty friend is now eating goldfish crackers, the crumbs stick to the snot on his face. It's disgusting.

Standing still again.

"Will you marry me?" was the first thing Padati ever messaged me. It made me laugh, so I answered him. We had a nice conversation that day… and every Tuesday after that day. Shortly after we started video chatting, I fell in love… we fell in love. We talked every day, about what life is like for him, his religious festivals, and the beautiful symbolism of everything he does.

For me, every day is the same. John and I get home from work, he plays on the Xbox and I read or knit. Every. Single. Day. We don't even go out anymore. There's no sex. No children. We don't even go out to eat. There's nothing. I can't go on like this. My husband is my child. I'm doing the right thing. I'm sure of it. Yes, yes, the right thing. He'll be better off without me. I'll be better off without him. He can go find some childish adult from his stupid gaming forums, he'll be happier. And, I'll be with the man of my dreams, my Prince Charming, Padati. The child sneezes, snot and crumbs hit my face. Fan-fucking-tastic!

The line stops moving again.

"So, where are you going?" The mom in front of me tries to start up a conversation with a demure smile on her face. She's very pretty in her traditional light-blue sari, flowing dark hair, and caramel-colored eyes that shine brightly against her darker skin. The teardrop shaped rhinestone bindi on her forehead accents her eyes perfectly. Gold bangles line her forearms. She wears large hoop earrings almost as big as the bangles. She looks exotic. In fact, she looks completely out-of-place standing in the middle of the most boring airport in D.C. The only connection to her from this earth is the snot nosed, goldfish encrusted child on her hip. Her husband is dressed more blandly, white button-down shirt, black pants, and sandals.

The line is still not moving.

"Oh, I'm flying to Mumbai," I answer. Her face goes into a smile.

"Interesting," she says in a thick Marathi accent. "Are you going for business?"

I don't look like the average business person, I am quite the opposite. There's nothing stunning about me, but Padati thinks there is, which is one of the reasons I love him so much. He tells me I'm beautiful every chance he gets. My husband doesn't even notice me anymore.

"No, not for business, I'm meeting a friend."

"Okay, good. Is she meeting you at the airport?"

"He. And yes, he is."

"He. Oh okay." She looks at me oddly as she looks down at my wedding ring. "I guess it's a good thing, you wouldn't want to be a white woman on your own in Mumbai."

"What do you mean?" She doesn't answer me as she turns her back to me once more. Was she judging me? What did she mean about being a white woman on my own?

Everyone in the line takes two steps forward.

I stand in silence again, trying not to think about the abrupt end to our conversation. I start fiddling with my wedding ring. How long will it take John to notice I'm gone? I wrote a note, but he won't notice it. Not explaining wasn't the classiest move I've ever made, but I can't tell him in person. He's a good person, this will tear him apart, I don't want to see that. I can't see that. Writing a note was the best thing for me to do. It's just… easier… for me. Someone has lost their passport; the line is at a dead stop now.

I remember one time when I posted a new profile picture online, Padati texted right away telling me how beautiful my green eyes were. He wanted us to video chat so he could really see my eyes. We talked on Skype that night for hours. I still remember the conversation so clearly.

"Baby, there you are!" he said to me with a very thick accent.

"I'm here!"

"Beautiful eyes," he said while smiling into his camera. "When can I meet you? I have to meet you." I felt surprised by this question, I thought he was just someone fun to talk to. Someone to give me a little bit of excitement. Someone to think about in this boring world. I wasn't expecting to actually meet him.

Photo by Shashank Sahay on Unsplash

"Oh, I don't know." I didn't know what else to say.

"You come to India, it's beautiful here." The background image I was seeing looked old, paint was peeling off the walls, and it was small. So small. Little matter though, he's a business executive, he makes money.

The longer we talked, the more I forgot about anything other than him. It didn't bother me that his living conditions were so different from mine. He

wants me! A middle-aged, boring American woman. He is so exotic and I'm so boring. Of course, I fell in love with him. He could have any woman he wants, but he wants ME! The little boy points to me and waves, he's adorable, in spite of the snotty crumbs still stuck to his face. Why doesn't someone wipe his face? The line begins to move again.

Padati and I started talking once a week through Skype. I began to forget his accent while he started teaching me some Hindi. He taught me all about his Hindu festivals and parades, it all sounds so otherworldly. He quickly became the person I think about when I wake up, and the person I think about when I fall asleep. Everything about him seems like a dream.

"If you come to India, you will love it!" he says with a smile that could light up a thousand Earths.

"I've never thought of going to India before."

"Baby, you must see all of this." He pans his phone around the street. Everything is beautiful, everyone is tossing flowers on top of each other. Two large statues of Krishna and his wife are being pulled down the street as people crowd around dancing while rose petals flutter down on top of them. Everyone is having so much fun, I want to be a part of it. I want to be a part of his life. The Pushpa Abhishek festival looks so amazing, I told him I would be there for it the next year. It's a week away now, I smile to myself. I stand, waiting to go to him in India, just in time for the festival I was so excited to see. It's absolutely perfect. More people get in line.

John never notices who I am talking to, that's how invisible I am to him. All he cares about are his games and gaming friends. I'm only there to cook for him, wash his clothes, run the vacuum and dust. It's the same conversation every night.

"Can you make something for dinner for once?"

"Pizza or Chinese?" He moves his face towards me, his eyes still on the screen.

I sigh, whispering profanities under my breath realizing the laundry has been piling up.

"Can you help me carry the laundry downstairs?" I grasp for straws.

"Can't you just throw it down the stairs instead of carrying it? It would be easier." He is annoyed and shooing at me while playing his game.

I stare at him for what feels like an hour. I get no reaction.

He barely talks to me, nor I him. I'll admit I had dreams of leaving long before I met Padati. Padati convinced me to leave but it didn't take much convincing, I'll admit. There is a confused elderly couple at the counter that doesn't speak English. The line is stopped.

The beautiful mother turned around to me again. "Is your friend an American? Is he your husband?" Her stunning eyes look at me again, all the while trying to wrangle her children.

"He's Indian." I don't answer the second question. I start fiddling with my wedding rings. Why didn't I take these off?

"Oh." She looks at my rings again. "Is he an old friend from school?"

"No, no, more recent than that." I'm still fiddling.

"Just, be careful. There is a big difference between America and India, you know."

"Leave her alone," her husband snaps. She rolls her eyes at him and starts yelling at him in Hindi.

Her youngest son, still on her hip, starts to wave at me. I wave back. The line starts moving. They are next in line.

Still fiddling with my ring, I think back to two weeks ago. Being stuck in my bed with the flu was not fun. Every time I stood up I felt like my legs would buckle under the pressure. John made sure to bring me drinks and soup. He also held a cold compress on my forehead to try to get the temperature down. Each time he left he would kiss me on my forehead. He can be a giving man sometimes, I just needed more than he could give. I'm doing the right thing. He'll find someone that really appreciates him. This will be good for him. It will be good for the both of us. I just realized I'm still twisting my wedding rings. I should really take them off. The line is stuck as someone argues about the weight of their bags.

Think about Padati, only about Padati. You've gotten this far into your new life, the rest is easy. The new culture will be interesting. Living with him, his mother, and two sisters in a two bedroom apartment in the middle of Mumbai. It will be… fun. My three bedroom townhouse may have seemed suffocating sometimes, but his apartment sounds…well… quaint. Still fiddling with my rings, I look around me, families everywhere. There's a honeymooning couple half way through the line, holding hands and giggling. I remember when John and I went to Hawaii after our wedding, we acted exactly like the couple in line. I was so happy then, he was happy. Mr. and Mrs. Ryder, with not a care in the world. I remember my horrible sunburn, he made sure to put lotion on me and call room service. When we swam in the warm ocean water, he held me close as we bobbed up and down in the waves. I had never felt so close to someone else in my entire life. We were both so happy, I was sure I would grow old with him.

The line begins to move again.

My breath quickens, I feel flushed. Suddenly my first kiss with John comes to my mind. We were on the docks at Fell's Point, it was night and we had just finished dancing, completely drunk and practically tripping over each other. The stars were out, and the sounds of the harbor were beautiful. He grabbed me and kissed me at that moment. It was a deep kiss…the most amazing kiss I had ever experienced.

The family in front of me moves to the counter. Now it's just me at the front of the line. The little boy waves goodbye. I smile. I take a few steps forward while the rest of the line follows behind me.

I don't think I can get these rings off my finger, they are stuck. The family in front of me starts loading their suitcases onto the scale, the little boy is standing next to his mom now, still watching me. The mother picks him up, once again. The whole family wisps away toward the security line. I hear the little boy say "bye-bye" in a thick accent. It's time for the line to move again. It's my turn at the counter. My rings won't come off.

I stand still. I'm frozen. The woman behind the counter looks frustrated with me. It feels like ten minutes go by, people around me start to complain. Suddenly, I'm not so sure. I can't take a step. Padati is gorgeous, he loves me, and we click, but another culture? I've studied India, sure, but could I be there for the rest of my life? I thought about this a million times, but suddenly I'm scared. I haven't really worked on things with John. I wonder if we could bring the passion back? But Padati is going to be waiting for me at the airport in Mumbai. I stand a little while longer as the people around me become more and more up-set. I have to make a decision and I have to make it now. I pick up my bags, strap on my back-pack, and begin to take a step towards my future.

Photo by Olekandr Pidvalnyi from Pexels

52

Downward Spiral
Ayo Gutierrez

It was totally unexpected,
   to say the least
   when your
   happiness
   was sapped,
   and Sadness
   crept over your
        countenance.
   You were living the life
   Borderless
   Sky was the limit
   A quintessential bachelor
        who once wore the diadem
   of massive success
   at a breakneck speed
   I watched you from a distance
   but closely
   How the yesteryears
   carried on a dark plot
   that twisted your fate
   A juicy canard
        casting your entire kin
     full of clandestine affairs
The stigma
        of a bastard
   spread rapidly
     like a
     forest
     fire.

The flames swallowed
your every reason to live.
   A tattered soul
   was left
        that breathes
   through the nostrils
   of shame
   and confusion.
   I missed seeing
        your auburn eyes
        once beaming with pride.
        Now dull with a sickening coldness--
permeating
your entire being.
How your taciturn demeanor
        endears you to the creepy
        and nocturnal creatures.
        The moon your regular patron...
        You
Pounded
     Screamed
     Howled
And fought your
Faceless Foe
Day after day
   Year after year...
   In the same spot
   where you chose
to end
   Everything
   AT
        L A S T.

Patterns
Michael Recto

Nicole loved patterns. Routines put her at ease. As long as the patterns are followed, all would be well in Nicole's world. Nicole, however, was no stranger to the occasional flaws in her regimented lifestyle. She woke up at exactly 6:45 am and got up on the right side, not the left, ensuring that her right foot, not her left, touched the floor first. She took a shower with cold water, tapped the door knob seven times before leaving the bedroom, and avoided the last step as she descended the stairs, just like always.

She had breakfast and browsed through the news on her smartphone while facing east. But all morning, she had an inkling that she deviated from a pattern she needed to follow. After entering her car, she tapped the transmission seven times and jangled her keys before inserting it into the ignition, just like every day. She never dared to mess the pattern up. She just couldn't.

On the road, she counted every signpost she saw and drove around seven blocks before parking in front of her office building. Neglecting her weekly Tuesday ritual was preposterous to her. She had to do it. She needed to. And yet, a persistent doubt followed her like a shadow. Something was missing!

When she reached her office table, she took out a bundle of pencils from a drawer and arranged them in perpendicular rows before her. She then ran her hand through them, sending them into disarray, and then picked them up one by one to be bundled up again and shoved back into the drawer. Her hands shook as she turned on her office computer. That same dreadful sensation lingered. Nicole couldn't shake off the anxiety that she forgot a pattern. She tore a page from the calendar that hung on her cubicle and stared at the date. Seventh of July.

After typing a short email, she took the bundle of pencils from her drawer, walked a short distance to her boss's office, and closed the door behind her.

"Need anything Nicole? I read your email," asked her boss with an inquisitive look.

"I just miss you," answered Nicole. Her boss stood up and leaned forward for a kiss. Nicole then held a fistful of the man's hair and rammed a pencil straight into his carotid artery. She smiled as she watched the horrified look in her boss' eyes.

"It's so funny that you were just like them." Nicole giggled as she remembered the chef who she gouged with a chopstick last February, and the electrician who she punctured with a screwdriver last March. Nicole then slammed the bloodied man's head seven times against his office table. The dull thumps of his shattered skull was nostalgic to her. It was like that college kid's head against his Mustang's hood last April, and that cute janitor's skull against a boiler room pipe last May. They all made the same cracking sounds, the same muffled screams, and the same pathetic moans.

Patterns are beautiful, aren't they?

The next morning, Nicole woke up at 6:45 am, got up on the right side of her bed, avoided the last step on the stairs, had breakfast and read a headline on her smartphone while facing east.

"Seventh Day Serial Killer Strikes Again."

Nicole loved patterns. Rituals made her happy. As long as the patterns are followed, all would be well in Nicole's world.

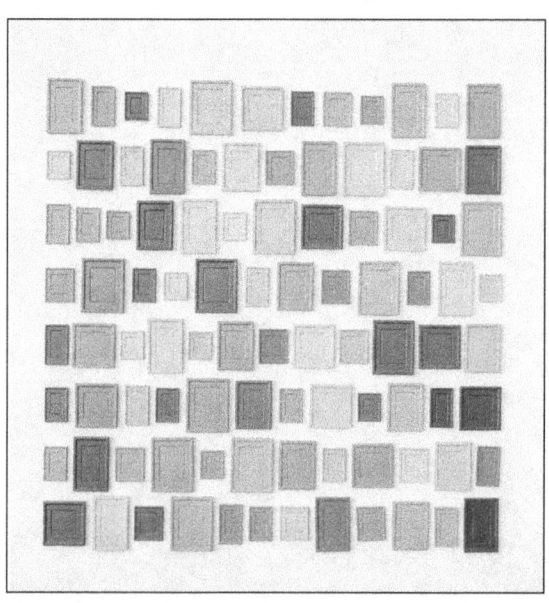

Photo by Markus Spiskeon on Unsplash

A poem from The Water Logs
KMJVB

Until the skies split and divide,
the stars shine for you,
Silas......
Nevermore will they hide,
they glitter because you do,
It's true.......
Gold, silver and blue.
I missed the train again....
but that's okay,
The next one came, as it always does,
....It came with the rain.

Devil's Little Sister
M. Lynn Valle

Anti-Social you say? You DARE to label me?
You should be thankin' me.. for my public service.
Doc, c'mon ya gotta believe me… ALL This cloak and dagger shit?
Nah… not really my swagger. Listen what you don't know could hurt you.
You have NO IDEA how much… Just so you know I never deserted you…
not like that.
Open your eyes to see OR close them…
however you need them to be trackin' this vibe.
The method to my rhyme… it may be RANDOM to you,
BUT in MY mind it makes perfect sense.
I guess what I'm tryin' to say is… my demons find me on any given WEAKDAY
and I am the ONE who is chained, at my OWN request.
I know, you're STILL scratchin' your head and cockin' it to the side; winking one EYE.
Can't help but think about why does this make ANY sense?
Or even HOW?
Because, Doc, that's the ONLY way I can express my LOVE
to the people who matter to me. The ones who ever gave a shit ABOUT me.
I just stay AWAY while my demons come out to play...
my ULTIMATE SACRIFICE IS to be away from those who LIVE in my HEART

Photo by Alexander Krivitskiy from Pexels

56

Red Meat
S.L. Ramero

"I come to you as human,
not just a reporter.
I know not how much time I have
before I, too, succumb.
All around me has been lost.
To any who survive from here on out,
know that our answer has become
the problem."

The recording is playing on the television for the tenth time this hour—a solemn reminder of what's to come for Carter. His inner thoughts have run rampant for the past three days, preparing for when he succumbs like the others. Everything he has done throughout that time has revolved around surviving for as long as possible.

Air conditioners turned off, windows taped shut, every crack and crevice (albeit doorways and drains) blocked, he has locked himself away from the outside world simply to prolong his lifespan.

It's inevitable. Peering through his barricaded apartment window, he watches while humanity devours itself.

Meat. Looking back to the world before, he can safely say it was a false necessity. The animalistic growling and screeches of those who wander the streets are the only music that has played in the three weeks since the end of the world. Silence he seeks. In silent yearning he attempts, yet fails, to muster up courage. To ignore their cries for fear of being alone. Ever since the beginning of this apocalypse, with everyone running from the first cannibals, some of which fell victim instantaneously, the harmonizing screams have continued to stand in preference to the quiet.

Down below him and across the street, a group of small children, no older than ten, are attacking each other with their teeth. Biting into each other's flesh, they paint the sidewalk in pints of blood.

From his second story window, he has seen it all; from men to women to children eating each other. Even infants are no longer safe from humanity's devolution into this primal nature. The thought itself is sad and it left him in a state of mourning for the remnants of the human race.

"Three weeks ago, scientists attempted to solve the global issue for the endangerment of cattle with a prototype pheromone created to initiate sex drive as a means of mass production.

They succeeded."

"Tragic," he whispers to himself. Inhaling deeply, he continues to watch. These kids should be playing and having fun. They should be riding bikes, enjoying the park, playing games. Not… this.

Carter turns his back against the window, refusing to further witness the carnage. He looks upward and sighs. What will he do when the world goes cold? He cannot adapt or salvage the last of the living. Is this for our crimes? Our sins against nature?

Silence remains his answer a moment longer, followed quickly by anger. "GOD DAMMIT!" He reaches for a coffee mug and throws it across the room. "What the hell do you want from me?!"

A crash resonates from the bathroom, obtaining his attention, then the door bursts open to reveal a child smothered in blood. She releases a blood-curdling screech and charges towards him, with each step leaving behind footprints of blood—and toenails.

Carter looks away, knowing he is hallucinating again. For 24 hours the visions have been coming and going, each one getting worse. He forcibly squeezes his eyes shut, listens to the pounding in his ear.

A second glance toward the bathroom door reveals nothing but dry floors and cracked wood along the surfaces.

"The world rejoiced at the thought of refilling its belly with red meat again. People all over dumped their fruits and vegetables in landfills and water resource areas.
To say humanity was ecstatic is an understatement."

Has the pheromone already reached him? Are these hallucinations one of the symptoms? Were it not for the growls coming from outside, Carter would find himself lost to such visions. Strangely enough, the cannibals have kept his mind in check by reminding him of his humanity.

Maybe now he is losing it.

He shakes his head and rubs the sweat off his face, breathing heavily between his fingers. The growls of the infected grow in numbers, seemingly surrounding him in their voices. A pounding in his head emerges, signaling a severe migraine to follow. A flicker of movement in the corner of his eye causes him to turn. Behind him appears a blonde woman with a smile on her face. She leans towards him with her lips hovering close to his own. She mouths incomprehensible words, but he senses he can understand them.

"I don't know what to do anymore," he whispers to her. "Things just aren't what they used to be. They're so much worse. We've gone from fighting each other over cows to completely destroying anything living. I don't want to step outside… I can't. The moment I walk out of this building, the last of humanity dies."

"Government scientists said they studied for every possible outcome. From how the pheromone affected other mammals, insect life, even plant life. Everything checked out."

Carter turns back to the window. More cannibals lunging at one another to satisfy their undying hunger. Teeth biting off large portions of skin, fingers digging out eyes and scalping weaker individuals.

Feeding like wild dogs. Every last one of them.

Reaching for her hand he asks, "Did it hurt? When you turned, did you feel any pain?"

Silence.

His fingers close over empty air, and this time when he looks back to her he sees pieces of flesh missing. Lips gone, a severed breast, flayed fingers; what is leftover is smothered in blood. Tips of her

formerly gorgeous hair are bathed in red, dripping to a puddle at her pale feet.

"I can't handle that. I can't handle any of this… not anymore. I thought I could survive but…" This time he successfully grabs her hand, "This is killing me. I don't want to be alone but I don't want to die either. Where do I go from here?"

"What they failed to do was test how this pheromone influenced human behavior. Within three days of its release, noticeable changes began to occur. Reports from numerous cities across the U.S. revealed hundreds of thousands of murders."

Source: tock.tokapic.com

She locks her bony fingers into his own. He glances at the interlocked hands, feeling her tendons bleed onto his skin. But something throws him off. A searing pain courses through his palm and up his arm. It burns immensely, yet he cannot cry out in agony. It hurts as much as it feels sensational. He wipes away more of the sweat brewing on his brow and shuts his eyes for a second. Then he opens them to see the blonde has disappeared and he is left standing alone in the living room.

"I'm sorry, Claire" he mumbles.

It finally hits him: the hallucinations have not stopped for the latter part of the day. He is now convinced that the pheromone has reached him. Despite his efforts to survive the apocalypse, the time will come when he will have to join the rest of the human race in their cannibal ranks.

"I guess this is it," Carter whimpers. "I can't stop myself from becoming. But I don't want to go… Why did this have to happen? Fucking people just couldn't fathom the thought of living without meat for a few years. Every day somebody complains that their stomach isn't full. Gluttonous bastards. EVERY SINGLE ONE OF YOU! JUST SIMPLE-MINDED FAT FUCKS!"

The bathroom door explodes into splinters again, revealing a dozen small children—both boys and girls. Blood seeps from their mouths between their teeth and they charge toward him. He squeezes his eyes shut, ignoring the small taps of footsteps his mind forces him to hear.

Carter slaps himself over and over. "Enough, enough, enough! No more!"

"Most news stations gathered the information as just another day in our fucked-up world. Until elaborate details of the attacks were released, unveiling gruesome cannibalistic individuals for each and every crime."

The growling children surround him, spitting blood as they do so.

He presses his palms into his temples in aggravation, "Stop! This isn't real. None of you are real. This is all the pheromone. Just please…stop." The children screech. They grab him and tear away at his flesh.

"STOP!" Carter screams as they peel off bits and pieces. There is nothing he can do to stop them, some of which feel like they have the strength of adults. Overwhelmed by the pain of being eaten alive, he falls over and succumbs to their whims.

One by one, they bite into him, scratching at the skin. A small child digs out his eyes while another scalps him. His toes are bitten off with crunches. And he feels everything.

"A week past Day One, scientists announced the pheromone as the reason for these attacks. Slowly but surely, it triggered a form of intelligence deterioration in humans, devolving them to an animalistic primitive nature."

The pain ceases immediately. Everything has gone back to the way it was before the children showed their faces. No broken bathroom door or blood, only the voices of cannibals, wandering outside the apartment.

Carter stands to his feet with a blank expression. He looks around somewhat confused, his eyes rolling around like he does not know his surroundings. The air feels thinner than before, leaving a stinging sensation in his chest with every breath.

Walking to the window, the floorboards creak under the pressure of his footsteps. He looks outside to observe the voices of the lost, each one grabbing at each other to feed the insatiable hunger.

The cries of those devoured did not give him even the slightest bit of discomfort or sympathy; he merely watches with curiosity.

"People fed on each other, driven by the basic need to consume anything in plain sight. Ten days after Day One, most of the world's infrastructure collapsed and life began to cease moving forward. Those with some humanity

left fled to churches and bunkers."

A few moments pass. Carter turns away and walks to the cabinet near the kitchen sink. He grabs an unopened can of peaches and places it on the counter by the knives. Grabbing the largest knife of the bunch, he punctures a hole into the top of the can and cuts into a semi-circle. Without a second thought, he pulls the lid backwards with his bare fingers and begins to eat. The sweet savory taste of the fruit leaves a tingle in his mouth. The juices that flow down the back of his hand makes his skin shiver with a familiar feeling.

He walks back to the window with the peaches in hand and stares outside.

"The government fell alongside more than half the population. Those of us that are still sane knew that this would be it. Our solution to a man-made problem became the issue that we would never solve."

Halfway into the can he pauses, pulling back his lips to bare his teeth. Remains of the fruit seep over his lips. The sting in his chest disappears for a few seconds as he munches on his food.

"Know that some tried to fix this but they didn't have enough time. And with that, these now become man's final hours. To any that are still alive: good luck and God bless."

Carter looks into the can to see two peach halves left. Grabbing both, he shoves them into his mouth and chews them to a pulp.

Switching his gaze back and forth between scenarios unfolding outside, he sees multiple groups still eating each other. A few others fight for dominance at the chance of having a full stomach.

Carter only smiles and continues chewing the last of his peaches. The taste isn't as sweet as when he first opened the can. The flavor resembles more that of bland copper. The texture has changed somewhat—simultaneously dryer yet juicier.

Crunch. That last bite clearly had part of the pit in it.

Carter uses his free hand to wipe away the juice, the back of it coming off red. He glances down to see blood at his feet. Staring at the bloody stubs remaining on his hand, he wonders what happened to his fingers.

Her Dark Journey
Rebecca Kapjon

Belle drives down a dirt road hoping to find the small, quaint town in the brochure sitting on the seat next to her. The Jeep starts to chug and sputter, giving her grave concern as she pulls to the side of the road. The headlights illuminate the pitch-black road ahead of her, surrounded by large trees and bushes. Belle looks at the gas gauge and realizes it is on empty. When she started the trip, the tank was full. She should have had more than enough gas to get to the village. She shakes her head as the car stalls, slamming her fists into the steering wheel as it lets out a loud beep. Even the horn sounds sickly, she thinks.

At this rate, she is never going to make it. This trip is supposed to be a relaxing vacation at a beautiful country inn. The past few months have been horrible and stressful. Belle looks at her phone and, of course, there is no reception. She knew the cell service would be spotty out in the country. Just my luck she thinks, jumping out of the car and starting to walk down the dark, desolate road. She hopes a cottage is along the road, so she can ask for help or to use their phone.

The swaying of the trees and the darkness gives Belle an eerie feeling as she continues to walk along the road. She hears a rustling noise coming from the bushes along the road. She looks into the wooded area twice, thinking she sees a shadowy figure in the brush.

"Hello! Hello! I mean you no harm. I ran out of gas on the road and need help!"

She jogs in the direction of the shadowy figure as she yells.

"Hello! My name is Belle. Please help me."

The hair on the back of her neck begins to rise as she hears wolves howling in the distance. She runs through the woods to a clearing, spotting an old mansion. She rushes toward the gigantic house as the howling grows louder.

The cobblestone mansion reminds Belle of an old Victorian castle set in the English countryside from one her romance novels. She slowly approaches the front porch and uses the gold knocker to bang on the door. It eerily creaks open, as if by some unknown force, into the foyer of the house. Deciding to enter, she creeps into the living room, eyeing the cathedral ceiling. The place seems antiquated. After looking around for a moment, she begins to feel like she's traveled back in time. The full length windows are covered with red velvet drapes. The black, oversized couch and chair feel soft as she runs her fingers across the top. She continues to walk through the living room and comes to a stop near the bottom of the stairs. She hears sad organ music drifting down the stairs. The intoxicating and thrilling music summons her closer to the stairs. Standing at the bottom of the stairs, Belle sways to the sound of the sad song. She twirls around as the music starts to get louder and the tempo starts to increase.

***

Frederick's mouth waters as if seeing his last meal, as he watches the glowing creature walk through the door. He stands in the shadows of the living room, so he will not alarm her. He felt her presence on the road and needed to see her and feed off of her. He is not the type to use his powers for trickery but there was no other way to get her to stop on the road. Frederick smiles when he thinks about the defiant look on her face when the gas gauge read empty. In the woods he felt an undying urge to touch her and consume her the closer she came to him. He watches the woman's reaction to his serenade as he walks through the living room door. She is unaware of his presence in the room. After inhaling her lavender scent, he feels an overwhelming need to be close to her. Her chestnut brown hair is swaying as she dances to the music. He clears his throat to get her attention watching her dance with her eyes closed to the music. Belle opens her eyes and to her surprise a man is standing in the doorway.

"I'm sorry I walked into your home when the door opened. My car stalled down the road and I was hoping you could help me," Belle says sheepishly, wringing her hands together.

Frederick crosses the room in two quick strides to be at her side.

"Don't worry, I'm sure I can help you in some way," he says as he licks his lips.

He needs to control himself. Since the moment this woman arrived on the road his senses have been in overdrive. She is going to be trouble for him, but he needs her just the same.

"Tonight, why don't you stay here with me and we will look at your car in the morning," Frederick says into Belle's ear.

She smiles, turning to look him. She tilts her head and gazes into his deep brown eyes.

"Are you sure my car will be alright on the side of the road?"

"It will be fine, my dear," says Frederick, guiding her up the staircase. "You look as if you have been traveling all day. Why don't you relax? I will have a bath drawn for you and then if you like you can turn in for the evening," says Frederick.

"I left my suitcase in the car. I don't have a change of clothes," replies Belle following Frederick down the hall.

"Don't worry, I have clothing from my mistress. You will be fine," says Frederick trying to convince her to relax.

Belle could use a bath and some relaxation after breaking down on the road. He is nice enough to offer her his hospitality. She should be gracious enough to accept it.

"I could use a nice relaxing bath," says Belle walking into the room at the end of the hall.

Looking around the room, the decor is the same time period as the living room. The room has a four poster canopy bed with drapes tied back to showcase a bed with lush pillows and blankets.

The wardrobe across from the bed is made of the same deep oak wood. On one side of the room is a vanity with a brush and makeup on top of it. A lit mirror is attached to the back of the vanity and a cushioned stool is tucked underneath. On the opposite wall stands a changing screen resembling those in old movies. Walking toward the bathroom, she continues through a powder room to a huge clawfoot soaker tub. Belle gazes at the man who is filling the bath. He is much taller than Belle, at least six foot with a slender build. His raven black hair is pulled back with a dark colored ribbon. It hangs to his shoulders, and she smiles thinking of his deep brown eyes. Frederick hunches over the tub as it fills with water, adding bubble bath for her pleasure. He keeps checking the water to see if it is the correct temperature.

He turns to look at her, "My apologies. I forgot to get your dressing robe," remarks Frederick. He walks past her and rummages through the wardrobe. He gives her a full length red silk robe and nightgown.

"Thank you," says Belle at a loss for words, "I'm so sorry, I forgot to tell you my name. I'm Belle. What is your name again?"

"I am Frederick, my dear. No need to apologize," says Frederick.

Belle walks behind the changing screen and starts to change into the robe.

"I thought I had enough gas to get the village when I left my apartment. I feel so stupid for running out on the way. I would have filled the tank when I passed the last gas station," says Belle.

Frederick feels Belle's presence in the bathroom before she walks into the room. He stands up and looks at her in the red silk robe.

"You look beautiful in red," says Frederick as he walks closer to Belle.

He raises her arms from at her sides so he can look at her entire body. She is a petite woman with shoulder length chestnut colored hair. Her blue eyes sparkle from the light in the bathroom. Frederick wants to pull her into his arms and kiss her lips and neck. He looks into her eyes and can feel her longing for him. He needs to walk away from her and let her decide whether she wants to find him. He needs to let her decide if he is what she is looking for on her journey. Frederick releases her arms and walks toward the cabinet. He removes two big towels and gives them to Belle. Bending over the bathtub, he checks the temperature of the water and turns the water off.

"The bath is ready for you. Please make yourself comfortable. I will be downstairs if you need anything," says Frederick.

He looks at her one last time before leaving the room and proceeds down the stairs. Approaching the living room, there is a shadowy figure lounging on the couch waiting for his arrival.

"How long have you been here?" asks Frederick as he sneers in her direction.

"Long enough to know you have a tasty treat waiting upstairs. Please tell me you have tasted her. She looks delicious," says the shadowy figure as she gets up from the couch.

"She is none of your concern, Dahlia. When and how I feed is none of your business," Frederick sternly says.

"My love, you know I only care about your well-being. It has been far too long. I'll never understand why you don't look at them for what they are: food," says Dahlia.

"This one is different. I can feel a power in her like no other. With her by our side, we will be a powerful group," says Frederick.

"Remember, she is off limits."

Sulking into the other room, Dahlia looks over her shoulder.

"OH Frederick, when are you going to learn they are food. Don't deny yourself a good time. Go and have some fun with her or I will."

Frederick takes a deep breath as he looks toward the staircase in hopes of Belle coming downstairs.

Dahlia walks through the house to the back staircase. The girl is off limits. Don't touch her. He should know telling me she is off limits is like a green light. I am going to see this girl and see what is so

special. Dahlia walks up the back staircase to her room. She changes into an old staff uniform and walks into Belle's room. She watches the girl in the tub relaxing with a luffa in her hands. The water shimmers over her breasts and she can see her leg is slightly bent.

"Hello, my dear. Is there anything I can help you with?" asks Dahlia from the doorway.

Belle is startled by the woman standing in the doorway. Her instinct is to cover her body as the woman walks closer to the tub. Belle smiles hesitantly looking in the direction of the other woman.

"I'm sorry. I didn't know there was anyone else here. Is this your room?" asks Belle.

"No, I am here to help you with your bath. Were you able to find everything you need?" asks Dahlia as she takes the luffa out of the girl's hands.

Dahlia starts to brush the luffa over Belle's arms and reaches around her to wash her breasts. Belle goes to grab the luffa from Dahlia and turns to look at the woman.

"I'm fine. I don't need any help. I was about finished anyway," says Belle in a panic.

Dahlia gets the towel sitting on the chair next to the tub and unfolds it for her.

"Don't be shy. You are beautiful. Here: let me at least dry you off," says Dahlia with the towel in her hands.

"I can do it myself. Who are you?" asks Belle. "Frederick didn't mention anyone coming to help me. Are you a maid?" asks Belle.

"You are so full of questions. I am his friend, Dahlia. I will be down the hallway. I'm sure we will become good friends," says Dahlia.

Belle self-consciously wraps herself in the towel watching the other woman walk out of the bathroom and bedroom. What the hell was that all about? This place is strange. I should have never agreed to stay the night, thinks Belle as she changes into the nightgown and robe. She pulled the sash through the loops on the robe tying it tightly. She leaves the room, walking toward the staircase. She didn't want to give the wrong impression to Frederick. Belle continues to walk down the staircase gazing into the living area. It was as if he could sense her presence, he turns his head as she reaches the last step.

"Oh my dear, come over here and sit with me," says Frederick as Belle walks closer to the couch.

She sits next to Frederick and replies.

"I wanted to thank you for your hospitality. It is very nice of you to offer a room in your home. I promise as soon as I get gas for my car, I will be on my way."

"You can stay as long as you like," says Frederick as he reaches over moving a hair out of Belle's face.

Belle leans closer to him in order to feel his touch. She is in a trance, looking up into his eyes.

"You are to go up the stairs, ready the bed, and take off this robe. You will welcome me into your bed. I will be there in a few minutes. Go now, my dear," he says.

Frederick takes a deep breath and smells her intoxicating scent as she gets up from the couch. Belle smiles at Frederick walking up the stairs to the bedroom, in a trance-like state. Frederick looks down at his hands, taking a deep breath. He needs to go upstairs and take her, and then set her free. He needs to recharge himself, and the only way to do so is to lay with this woman. There is something different about her. She is not like the others who have passed through the town. He senses this. She has an aura about her which drives him crazy. Starting to walk up the stairs, he thinks: would it be terrible if he gave her the gift and made her like him? She would be a wonderful addition to his family. He cannot believe the overwhelming attraction he feels for her. He needs to be close to her and not just to feed off her. Being around her revitalizes his whole being and strengthens his senses. If she is to be like him, he needs her to choose to be like him and not be under his control.

Walking into the bedroom, she pulls the blankets down on both sides of the bed. She takes off the robe, hanging it on the changing screen. She sits at the vanity, brushing her hair and looking into the mirror, humming to herself waiting for Frederick to join her. She hears him walking down the hallway and gets up from the vanity. She sits on the edge of the bed and looks at the doorway as Frederick walks into the room. He walks up to her shirtless in silk pajama pants. He leans down and kisses Belle deeply as he crawls into bed with her. She wraps her arms around him as he pulls her close to him. He needs to take her in a way she has never experienced.

The Voyage
Edentu Oroso

Rise, great Muse, from the great spheres;
Show your hand in the craft of this art
    Guide the soft sail of this tall tale
    Lest in mortal memory, I weave not the Muse's craft
Bid your bud the scented sprout of wisdom,
As I weave time's threads in the voyage's loom.
    Retrieve anchor, turn the ship windward,
    Marvel, the roiling rolling towers of water
Seven, the sunlight sprays, seven, the blue blanket nights;
Of noise of silence, great voices of the Triangle
    Let me, great Muse, the splice of time to tell;
    Of the vaults of creation so suddenly slit
Of primordial voice, echo from the core of photons
To put to indelible ink the spirals of being
    Of gardeners, architects, engineers, etched in transit plains
    The sphere's chest of ageless intelligence
Remind me, great Muse, the holy howling of wind
Power horse of earth, in the banal romance with photons
And voice of aeons call in the depth of the wind;
Go, child of the realm, harness the free flood of ether
    And the deep to my wandering mind calls
    Earth's frame, soul and spirit, banished in the Triangle
Creation's till, chest of earth's enchantment
Yet, its placid vastness so deceptive
    Echoes from the deep, all of my pens drain
    Weaving the yarns of sacred secrets
So the permission, flood of vision, Triangle to leave
And the crew awoke in the passing haze.
The future tilled, and in the voyage sprouts
Sunshine ripened fruits, for those who seek.
And earth forms remain brimful thereafter.
So the decision to tell this tall tale

Of the shape of things to come.

The Lama
Neil Austin

The Lama sat in his tiny cell for a week, in darkness, waiting for his turn. Lacking sight, his hearing grew acute and he used it to build a virtual image of the cell block. There were ten cells opening off a corridor with a heavy door at the end. He knew morning from night by the rattle of keys opening that main door and the momentary band of light under his cell door. The quiet sobs and groans of the night froze at the sound of those keys. The heavy door creaked open, the strip of light brightened, then dimmed as the door clanged shut and weak bulbs came to life in the corridor. There were footsteps, a cell door opening. The sound of pleading, then thuds and screams. After that, it was quiet till the process was repeated the following day. He could see no pattern in the selection of victims for these beatings and he concluded the apparent randomness was simply another tool for maintaining terror. Red Guard efficiency.

***

The Chinese first entered Tibet via the eastern provinces of Kham. The warrior spirit of an older, wilder Tibet still sang in the veins of the Khampa nomads, and with the first rapes, beatings and murders by the occupying forces, that spirit awoke. Rebellious nomads gathered bows and arrows, ancient swords, and a few Lee Enfield rifles left behind by the earlier failed British mission. With these, they mounted a resistance. They were mosquitoes bothering the flanks of a tiger. By the time the army reached the Lama's monastery the violence had escalated well beyond the random excesses of soldiers. Control through terror was always the unwritten intent and it soon became official policy, as reflected in the systematic brutality of the new prisons.

The army arrived in clouds of dust. Over two days they filled the valley with the stink of diesel motors and the shouts of soldiers setting up camp outside the monastery walls. On the third day, they rounded up villagers and nomads that they might bear witness to Chinese authority. The soldiers hung speakers from the monastery walls and in raucous garbled Tibetan a Political Officer shouted and frothed his way through a bewildering speech.

China, the Motherland, has come to free the peasants from the yoke of Lamaist oppression. Liberation for the workers enslaved by the monasteries. Freedom from the monk class that grows fat on the people's labour.

The soldiers then entered the monastery en masse, bent on destruction. They ripped down thangkas, trashed altars, scattered offerings. They built fires in the courtyard and fed them precious texts, ancient woodblock prints and artworks. A thousand years of spiritual and artistic heritage trampled and burnt. They collected the statues of various Buddhas and Bodhisattvas, to pry out their jewels and melt down their gold. The fires burnt through the night. Screams and the occasional bark of gunfire drifted through the cold night air and echoed around the valley.

The apocalypse had come to Tibet.

In the morning the soldiers loaded the Abbot and senior Lamas on to the backs of trucks and paraded them, battered and bruised. Some of the younger monks shouted their protest only to be dragged out and beaten in front of the crowd.

***

The Lama had been recognized early in his

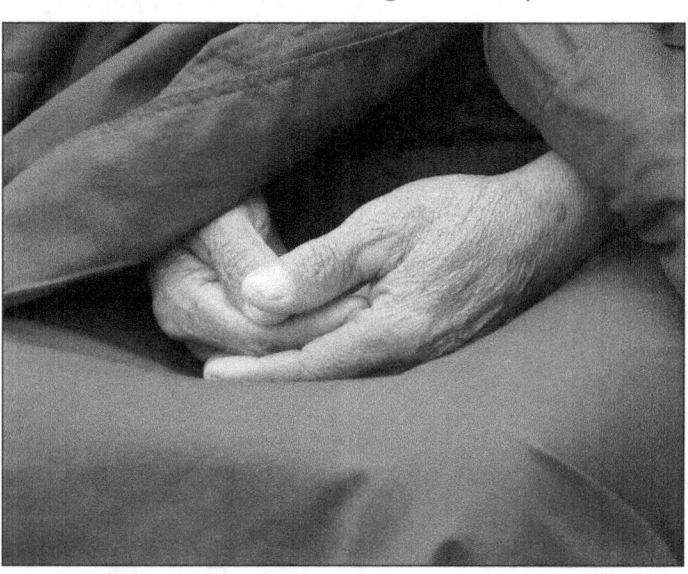

Source: Pixabay.com

life as the reincarnation of a great teacher. He was returned to the monastery at the age of 6, to be educated and to continue the work of his previous self. Now in his 50's, he had meditated his whole life. His intelligence and wit established him as a great debater in his youth, and later he gained renown as a teacher and occasional tutor to the Dalai Lama himself. He spent years in solitary retreat, sheltering in mountain caves, before returning to teach and write extensive commentaries.

The Lama embodied the true wealth of Tibet and as such, he was everything that the Chinese wanted to crush.

The first stage in the re-education of the masses involved the Red Guard targeting the high Lamas, mostly old men. The random daily beatings and 'struggle sessions' were part of the process of breaking them down. They were forbidden any images, their malas (prayer beads) were broken and scattered. If they were caught moving their lips in private prayer they were beaten.

Chairman Mao had called religion "The Opiate of the Masses" and the Chinese regarded Tibet as a superstitious and primitive backwater. They intended to wipe out Buddhism and replace it with communism, their own one true faith.

***

The morning began like all the others. The human sounds of the night immediately ceased as a clang of metal announced the arrival of the guards. The fear was palpable, sweeping through the cells. Whose turn would it be today? Each prisoner visualized the progress of the guards, three of them from the sound of their boots. The rising terror as they approached, the relief when they passed. The Lama waited, the boots approached, slowed, and stopped outside his cell. His heart beat like a drum as the fear took hold. Time dripped like slow melting ice. The guards were playing. They just stood there, outside his cell door, in silence. The Lama waited for the bolt to slide back. Nothing. Then, like a broken spell, the guards casually strolled on to his neighbour's door instead.

What the guards didn't know, could never comprehend, was that while they played out their perverse little game, a revolution was taking place in the mind of the Lama. In the darkness he was entirely focused on the door, acutely tuned like a cat focused on a mouse hole. Suddenly, within that crystal clarity, the thought arose: where is this focus when I try to meditate on emptiness?

The absurdity of this wayward thought, in this situation, struck the Lama like a blow. For as long as he could remember he had meditated on this riddle, seeking this thing called "the self", but he could not find it. The harder he tried to grasp the apparent self, the self the Buddha said was an empty illusion, the more it slipped away. Like mercury under a pin. Now, confronted with the terrible danger lurking outside his cell, the vision came to him of the guards attempting to beat up a ghost in a fog. The lama chuckled to himself.

In that instant, a flash of satori, and like a brilliant sun he was wide awake. His Bodhisattva heart was blown open in a rapture of clarity, the self-exposed for the complete illusion it always was. Everything in the Lama's life, his training, the endless hours of meditation, the accumulation of merit, everything had led to this shattering moment.

Oh, bliss.

Here, in this cell, the prison of self collapsed and the Lama was entirely free.

There was no time for celebration, though. With his own liberation assured, the Lama was acutely aware of the great danger now facing his neighbour. All fear of personal suffering had dissolved in the realisation of emptiness, but that fear was still very real for his neighbour. The Lama determined to save him from the imminent beating by taking it upon himself. Before the guard could pull the bolt on the cell next door, the Lama began a loud recitation of Chenrezig's mantra of compassion.

Om Mani Padme Hum
Om Mani Padme Hum
Om Mani Padme Hum

Taken aback by this obvious rebellion, the soldiers immediately returned to the Lama's cell and threw open the door. When they entered the Lama smiled, joined his hands in prayer, and greeted the first guard. "Tashi Delek." Infuriated, the guard lashed out with his baton and swept away the prayerful gesture. The first blow broke two of the Lamas knuckles. The second broke his nose.

The Lama had no idea how much time had passed when he came to in his cell. He did an internal survey. He was a mess, but alive. Satisfied, he propped himself against the wall and relaxed. He settled into the meditation techniques that were second nature to him and was soon in samadhi, a blissful state of one pointed concentration where pain was simply another sensation and no bother at all. His concentration was accompanied by great bliss and in the early hours of the morning, he received many visions.

Later the sun rose and the Lama waited patiently for the approach of the guards. Considering his situation, he was extraordinarily happy. All fear was gone, he was centred and overwhelmingly grateful. When the guards came he repeated his actions of the day before, loudly reciting his mantras. Drawing their attention and the subsequent beating onto himself he protected the others for another day. He kept this up for a week.

One morning his cell was silent. Curious, the guards opened the door. In the night the lama had propped his broken body against the wall, crossed his legs, and died in meditation pose. He wore a beatific smile, and a faint perfumed odour emanated from the body.

Moira
Benoit Chartier

Travis, the young store clerk who was helping him, had never seen the enormous thing before. Matthew ran his hand along the side of the old armoire, the smoothness of the deep brown varnish slipping under his fingers like lukewarm ice, if such a thing could be possible. After having left Matthew in admiration of the ancient thing, he returned with a manager. Matthew had had the time to open it, take in the smell of horse-carriage and mildew, encyclopedias and hand-washed linen. And something else.

The grey-mustached man frowned as he approached, an eyebrow cocked at the hulking shape of the furniture, which, in a new furniture store, looked alien and unwelcome among more modest pieces. Matthew had spotted it from across the floor, standing as it did between a loveseat and full-length sectional, like a monolith dropped in from some other dimension.

Photo by Kaique Rocha from Pexels

He knew he could have stood easily inside it, but he felt vaguely uneasy when he got too close to the far drawers on the right-hand side of the contraption. He chalked it up to lack of sleep. Being a new father had its perks and drawbacks, and resting only half any given night was most assuredly on the drawbacks side of the equation.

Whatever he might feel about its interior, he needed this fine piece. He wanted something classic to go in his little girl's room, and this was it. The grey-mustached man, who reminded him of a thinner Wilford Brimley, stalked around the thing, smiling to himself whenever Matthew looked in his direction, but inspected the inside with minutiae the instant his gaze went to some other part of the store, or Travis distracted him.

In the end, he agreed to part with it for the low sum of two thousand dollars, no extended warranty, and Matthew managed to talk him down to sixteen hundred. Travis walked away, sulking. Wilford Brimley's look-alike, or 'Mr. Foster', as his nametag claimed, filled in paperwork in his office as Matthew looked on, picturing him saying diabeetus, and thinking what a wonderful addition it would be to Joy's room. Right opposite her crib, next to the window.

His wife Laura looked at pictures he'd taken and sent to her phone, pouting, as he returned. Joy lay in the crook of her arm, fast asleep. Matthew looked at Laura's and Joy's short blonde hair and smiled.

"What is that thing?" she asked, holding the phone up for Matthew to see.

"Her new closet, love. It's got a lot of history!" He walked behind her and kissed her ear.

"That tickles! I didn't think you'd get an antique. It must have cost a fortune," flipping from one picture to the other, zooming in on the detailing.

"That's the funny part. I don't think they knew what kind of treasure they had. I got it practically for a song. A short one."

She shrugged and gave him a peck on the cheek.

Two days later, the delivery men came to the house, removing the front door to fit it in. They lowered it so it could come in horizontally, and both large men held one of the doors closed so that they not get caught in the wooden bannister as they climbed the carpeted stairs to the second floor.

As they hoisted the cumbersome piece up the first five steps, the leading man's grip slipped, and the cabinet fell backward toward his partner. The unexpected extra weight made him lose his handhold, and the massive piece of furniture dropped, hitting him square on the knee. They heard a tearing, breaking sound, and the man shrieked in pain. Laura ran to the kitchen with Joy, calling nine-one-one as she did. Matthew bolted to the man's side, gripping the underside of the closet with both hands and tried to lift it, with no luck. The man sat on the floor, pushing against the armoire to no avail, it crushed both his legs and pinning him, his eyes wide and cries of pain deafening. His partner remained stuck up the steps, unable to come down without stepping on top of the heavy furniture and injuring his partner further.

Matthew ran to the garage and grabbed a two-by-four left over from the renovations of the backyard fence and rushed back into the living room. He jammed it under the armoire and lifted the wooden lever as hard as he could, allowing the trapped man an inch or so of space to wiggle away from the enormous thing.

When Matthew dropped the two-by-four, it slapped to the ground with a thud, and the injured man's partner leapt over the offending furniture as fast as he could, coming to the other man's side. The wailing of the ambulance came not five minutes later, and as the EMTs lifted the sobbing man, his leg hung limply, threatening to fall off.

The other delivery man stayed behind long enough to right the armoire, his face red and the vein on his temple pulsing, and push it into the living room, before excusing himself, out of breath, promising to send another team to bring it upstairs when time permitted, as he rushed off to the hospital, chasing his partner.

Laura sat in the kitchen, crying, and baby Joy, sensing her mother's anguish, imitated her. Matthew could only sit next to both of them, putting his arms around his wife and saying, "There, there. It'll be okay."

His heart beat an army roll-call, a cadence he knew would give him an attack if it didn't slow down.

"That poor man," she said.

"It'll be alright," he answered, his smile not quite covering up for his terrified eyebrows.

There was no blood on the floor, or anything that could attest to this terrible event. It was almost as if it'd never happened. The furniture store had called two hours later and promised to send another crew in the morning to get the piece to where it was supposed to be. They apologized for any upset, but it was the man the couple was upset about. They assured them that he would be fine, but Laura and Matthew weren't foolish enough to believe it.

Matthew walked around the closet to assess damage, but there did not seem to be any. Whoever had built it, had built it to last. Nothing constructed today would have withstood the fall, but on the other hand, the man would not have been injured so badly, or so Matthew thought, beginning to throw blame on himself. Even the two right feet, which had bashed against the floor of the landing, had not even suffered a scratch, to his relief and consternation.

He played with the door to see if the hinges had suffered. As he opened and closed it, a slip of paper fell to the ground. He looked behind him, but Laura must have been downstairs. It was yellowed, folded, and there was no doubt in his mind that it had been dislodged in the fall.

He opened it, and inside he found a drawing of a family. From the left, there was 'Daddy', 'David', 'Me', 'Mommy', and 'Dr. Pendlton'. The doctor's name had a little arrow pointing from between the 'l' and 't', to an 'e' that had been forgotten. The 'Me' was a little girl in a long dress. Before her feet, a large black dog, lay, his name 'Lucky'. All were smiling, but Matthew thought that Dr. Pendleton's was not as nice as the rest of the family's. He was the only one showing teeth, in a manner that reminded him of people wanting to show you as many pearly whites as possible to look trustworthy.

Matthew opened the closet door and placed the drawing on top of the drawers at the far-right. He wanted to show Laura, but felt that for today, she'd had enough strong emotions. Maybe tomorrow, if sleep permitted. Joy was indeed a joy, but he was looking forward to the day that she'd sleep an entire night.

In the early morning, he was woken from weird dreams of old closets tumbling down staircases to the sound of crying.

"My turn," he said to Laura, who muffled assent and stuck her face into her pillow. He half-stumbled out of their bedroom, rubbing his face, heading toward Joy's, when he realized that the crying had not come from the baby monitor beside the bed. He froze. Joy's room was straight ahead, maybe ten feet away. The crying came from downstairs, on his left. From the living room. It was faint. Not at all the newborn yowling he was used to. Older. More muffled.

"Hello?" he called into the darkness of the stairwell.

"Who's there?"

He listened. The weeping had stopped. Matthew's heart raced as he crept down the stairs. When he reached the fifth stair, a wailing startled him and he slipped, falling on his ass, making him slide all the way to the landing. Joy had woken up.

"I'm coming, Love!" he said, calling up the stairs.

Through the bluish moonlight coming into the living room, he noticed one of the doors to the armoire opening. His blood had been warming up again, but this made it turn marble cold. As Joy continued to cry, he walked, dream-like, to the cavernous opening of the closet, as if walking at the bottom of an aquarium.

As he set his hand to the wooden door, it felt oddly warm. Not burning, but body temperature. On the wooden back wall was a small door. Narnia, he thought, and he would have smiled if he hadn't been so terrified. His trembling hand reached out, and turned a clasp that held it closed. The door fell open toward him, clacking on the bottom of the armoire. Matthew's head shook 'no', as he plunged his hand in the sucking darkness of the back wall. He felt… something, and pulled it out. It was round, like a hard necklace.

Matthew pulled his sweating head out of the closet and went upstairs to tend to Joy, and when he turned on the light in her room, he saw that

the thing he held was a dog collar, with the name 'Lucky' on the tag. He put it down on the changing table and picked up his daughter, rocking her slightly, as he brought her to Laura to be fed.

"Have you seen a dog collar in Joy's room?" he called out to her, the next day, as he knelt beside the changing table.

"Why would I have seen a dog collar? Do we have a dog I don't know about?" she answered from the kitchen. No, just the collar, he thought. As he was about to answer, his phone rang.

"Mr. Greenwald." The man's voice said. Not a question.

"Yes?"

"You purchased an item recently that was not for sale. There was a delivery mistake. We are willing to overlook any legal actions if you'll sell us the closet back. We'll give you twice as much as you paid, if that sounds satisfactory."

Matthew thought of the drawing, and the collar, and the delivery man's crushed leg, but there was this mystery surrounding the armoire that he couldn't shake. This feeling he'd had when he saw it from the other side of the room. Whether it was faint familiarity or something else, he did not know, nor cared.

"I'm sorry. I really like it, and want to keep it." The low rumble in the other man's voice shook him.

"You'll regret this, Mr. Greenwald! She's mine!" The click at the other end of the line startled him out of what felt like a trance.

When the new delivery men showed up the next day, he asked them to please place the closet against the far wall of the living room. He was keeping it, yes. Having it in his newborn daughter's room, however? That was an entirely different proposition.

"Is that where it'll live from now on?" Laura asked, her head askance, Joy in her arms and playfully chewing on one finger.

"I think so. For now." This massive wooden thing was like a yoyo in his mind. On the one hand, chills shrieked over his skin every time he came near, but he now realized it inhabited his thoughts at every waking hour, and sleeping hour to boot.

That night, when he heard the soft crying, he slipped to the first floor, padding down the carpeted stairs on the tips of his toes, cringing at every creak of the steps. There it was, on the far wall, waiting for him. His revulsion grew as he came closer, and the soft wailing diminished. As he reached out a hand to touch it, it ceased completely. Warm, like skin, he opened the door and peered inside. There was the tiny door at the back, and he undid the clasp, reaching into the darkened hole. As he groped in the darkness, he felt another door, at the far wall of the hidden compartment. He clicked on the pin that held it fastened and it, too, fell open.

He reached inside, and could feel the air getting colder, the further in he went. He turned his head and realized that he could barely make out the square shape of the first door, from which his slippered feet hung. How deep was this thing, anyhow?

Cold, moist air clung to him like midnight dew, flowering on his brow. He raised an arm, and felt his pajamas cling to him. Before his face, the rough feel of wood blocked his progress. Fumbling, he found another latch, and pulled it, a dim light illuminating his face from beyond.

Two men and a woman sat in a living room, in what must have been a museum. Some sort of co-splay from a hundred years ago. The lady wore an ornate dress, and her large-brimmed hat and bustle reminded Matthew of yellowed family photos. The men were also dressed appropriately for the time period. He noticed that one man and the woman sat on one side of a large desk, their backs to him, and the other man sat opposite, facing Matthew and the couple.

That man smiled with a full complement of white teeth, which he displayed to the couple.

"I'm afraid Moira is quite out of control, Mr. and Mrs. Merrill. After what she did to poor Lucky, I strongly recommend you place her. Angel House is willing to take her on as a patient, if you will trust us with her care," he said, after which his smile widened even more.

"I don't know what happened, doctor. Moira's not like this," the woman said, and Matthew noticed

for the first time that she must have been crying, her shoulders hunched.

"Ah, but insanity can strike swiftly!" the man they called doctor replied, making a stabbing motion with his hand.

"What will you be able to do for her?" the other man said.

"Keep her from harming herself and others. For now, that is the most that medical science can promise, I'm afraid," the doctor replied. As Matthew looked upon the scene, though, the doctor's gaze sharpened, and he peered between the man and woman he'd been speaking to. Matthew's eyes widened and he shut the tiny door, finding himself in pure darkness once again.

"What are you doing here?" a voice said, inches away from his face.

He screamed, backing away as fast as he could, shrugging his shoulders and wriggling his body. A cold breath followed closely, against his cheek, his forehead. His knees dropped down into the closet, and he whipped his head back, shutting the inside door as fast as he could, but not before seeing a pair of cold blue eyes in the dark.

The nightmare faded as he woke, but the eyes stayed behind his own. What are you doing here? Matthew shivered. Laura was cooking breakfast as he walked into the kitchen and sat down at the table.

"Morning, love," he said, but Laura didn't answer.

When she turned around from the stove, he detected the pinched look signifying he'd done something wrong. She was waiting for an apology.

"What's on your mind, dear?" he asked.

"She's not yours to keep, Matthew Greenwald. She's not yours and you know it. We're going to take her!"

She now stood a few feet away from him, her voice becoming more shrill. Joy was in her basket, near the table. She began to cry.

"Are you.." he began.

"GIVE HER TO US, GREENWALD, OR WE'LL TAKE HER AWAY!" she shrieked at him, and then went to Joy, her back stiff, hands fisted. She unclenched, picked up the baby, and Matthew got up from his seat, his arms out to Joy. When Laura turned around, though, she was busy tutting Joy and smiling.

"Morning baby, did you sleep well?" she said to Matthew.

"I… I… what?"

"Are you okay?" she said, bouncing Joy slightly in her arms.

"I'm… fine," he said, as he ran his hand through his hair.

A few nights later, when the soft crying began again, he tried to ignore it. The more he ignored it, the louder it got.

"Can you hear it, Laura?" he whispered to his sleeping wife. Her only answer an emphatic mmpph as she pulled the covers up to her neck. He tossed and turned, but the weeping grew louder and louder, as if it came from his own mind. He doffed off his duvet, and as soon as he set foot on the carpet, silence returned.

Matthew sighed and took a deep breath. It was dream state. All this wasn't real. He walked out of his room and slowly down the stairs. It came from below. The weeping. Quiet now. Muffled crying. Little gulps. It threatened to engulf him. Haunt him forever.

The doors were closed, but the warm skin feel of them was still there. He opened them with care, as if handling a newborn.

There, at the back of the cabinet, the tiny door. A kilometer away if it was a centimeter, and Matthew's mind reeled. His had reached out to it, and it begged to be opened.

Release me, it cried, in his mind. Save me!

Shaking, his fingers numb, he pulled the latch, the door clacking as it hit the lower part of the armoire. Wind like the sucking from a cave pulled toward the hole. An emptiness so vast that he might never return.

"Help me!" The voice cried from the void, and Matthew felt the desperation in it.

He reached into the cabinet, and his hands were gripped by small hands. So cold, yet he couldn't let go. Wouldn't let go.

"Moira!" He yelled into the darkness, and her face appeared before him, tears streaming from her bluish face.

"Matthew! What are you doing!" Came Laura's voice, from the landing.

Matthew turned around to tell her it was okay, but it was that man, that doctor, who stood where Laura should have been. He held Joy in his arms.

"Let her go, Matthew," he ordered.

Matthew turned toward Moira and felt the lump in his chest rising, the tears starting to fall.

"I'm sorry," he said, as he let the little girl go.

"Nonono! Don't! He's the one! He did it! Don't believe him!" she cried, her eyes in a panic.

"I'm sorry," he repeated, before letting her slip back into the void, and falling to the floor.

The little door closed on its own, slamming upwards with brutal force.

"Give me my daughter ba…" he began, turning toward the man who held his little girl hostage.

But he was gone, and so was Joy. Matthew got up on his hands and knees, scrambling to the base of the stairs in disbelief. He turned to the cabinet, but it had vanished without a sound.

"What? What?" he muttered, scrambling up the stairs on his hands and knees, almost slamming into Joy's bedroom door. The shape in the bed made him draw a sigh of relief, until he realized it was only her blankets. Joy had been taken.

Joanna didn't know what it was about the old cupboard she spotted at the furniture store, but thought it would look great in the kid's room. The middle-aged salesperson said he'd have to get the manager, as he'd never seen that piece in the store. She said it was fine. She was willing to wait. It was beautiful. It smelled of hand-washed clothing, old libraries and wooden flooring. There was something else as well, but she'd have plenty of time to find out what, and she smiled.

Aylah's Descent
Stephanie Neese

There was no way out. She'd been scraping at the dirt walls for hours to no avail, the hole was far too deep and the mud allowed her no grip to climb up the sides. She tried screaming but knew there was no one out in the woods this late at night to hear her. Why had she decided to go hiking alone at this hour?

Aylah curled up in the corner knowing there was nothing left to do but rest and wait for daylight. Sleep came fitfully and the chill of the damp made her shiver through her nightmares, dancing with the unnamed terrors of what would happen next.

She woke to the low deep growl of an animal. She sat up with a start turning her head toward the sound. That's when she saw it: a humanlike form crouched in a corner staring at her, covered in some sort of black sludge. It had bright red eyes and pinprick black pupils that burrowed into her soul. It stood in front of a door that had appeared in the muck of the walls. She could see the passage behind the snarling creature led down, into a depth where no human would come. The smell of sulfur drifted from the doorway, suggesting something evil deep within.

The sense that she had surprised the creature was overwhelming, giving her a moment of hope. This trap had not been laid for her. She jumped toward the creature at full force, grabbing it in a headlock before it could bite her with what looked like rows and rows of sharp, snake-like fangs gleaming inside a mouth that was much wider than she expected. Fortunately, the creature was smaller than she, approximately the size of a ten-year-old child. Although the black ooze made the hold slippery, the creature seemed to have an anatomy similar to a human. After an intense struggle, it passed out. As soon as it slumped to the ground she headed toward the small hole that the creature had crawled out of. She ignored the ebony slime that had stained her shirt and covered her arms, too scared to care.

It was dark, but down toward the bottom of the shaft she could see a faint red glow. A narrow ladder led the way down. She was in flight mode knowing the creature would wake again soon so she quickly descended the ladder made of some sort of volcanic rock. A part of Aylah's brain knew making her way into an unknown pit was probably a bad idea, but after seeing those rows of sharp teeth in that wide black mouth, there was no way she was waiting around for 'it' to wake up.

The smell of sulfur grew stronger and the walls were closing in on her as she worked her way down in the darkness. After what seemed like hours, but was probably only ten minutes, she heard a shrieking coming from far above her. The creature was awake. She started to take the rungs two at a time and every step down left a colder and colder feeling in the pit of her stomach. How could the tunnel go so deep? The shrieking started to sound closer and she was suddenly under the impression that whatever this thing was, it was fast on a ladder. The beast was gaining on her with a terrifying speed.

There was nothing left to do but let herself fall and hope for the best. The choice only took a moment but it required all of her self-control to let go of the ladder. The fall lasted only a moment, landing in a thick black stinking mud. She was submerged but could still hear the beast screaming down the tunnel so she held her breath and remained still. At least buried in this sludge it might not see her. The creature reached the end of the ladder, and dropped down to her left. It was slowly walking near her in the mud. She could discern a low growl and for a moment she thought she made out some sort of sniffing sound. Her lungs burned and she felt like there was movement in the mud around her, something slithering near her and rubbing against her arm…it was an effort for her not to move.

Just when she thought she couldn't hold still a moment longer the fiend let out a howl and she could tell the sound was headed away from where she lay. She burst out of the mud and took a deep breath full of hot, sulfur-filled air. It stung her nose and her eyes watered from the fumes. She looked around to find herself in some sort of wet cave, a dim red glow emanating from tunnels in several directions. In a panic, it suddenly dawned on her that the tunnel coming from the ceiling, the one that she came down through on the ladder, was nowhere to be seen. She pulled herself upright with an exerted effort: the fall into the mud had softened the impact but she could tell it had pulled muscles in her neck and back.

As she shucked ebony muck off of her arms, she felt a mass that was stuck. She pulled but it held fast, she could feel a sharp attachment that could only be some sort of massive leech. A leech as big as her hand. She tugged as hard as she could but it wouldn't budge. She pulled her hand away and, just as she did, the fist-sized black mass pulled apart like a pair of eyelids. Inside was a giant, red festering eye staring at her, which waved about wildly when it saw her. She instinctively poked her finger directly in the eye, stifling a scream and breaking into tears at the effort. The leechy thing flipped

Photo by Jose A. Thompson on Unsplash

around wildly and dove into the ground beneath her. The eye shut again. For a moment she watched as it swam through the mud toward the tunnels.

Despite her agonizing fear, Aylah felt her senses were as sharp as ever. She decided it was time to search for a new exit from this place before one of the horrifying monsters she had already seen returned, or a new one found her. She walked briskly toward the glowing tunnel closest to her, scanning the ceiling as she went… hoping to find another ladder out of there. This place. What was this chamber in the ground, and how was she going to escape?

As she moved cautiously down the passageway,

ankle deep in stinking black mud, she kept note of a variety of twists and turns. She wandered through a veiny network of dark glowing tunnels, all seeming to lead nowhere. Underground there was no sense of direction and it wasn't long before she felt completely lost. At this point turning around was no longer an option, and all sense of time evaded her. Had it only been minutes or had she been wandering these halls for eternity? It was dark. Every step she took left her fearful of what lurked in the soot beneath her.

She stepped into a large volcanic-looking chamber and the temperature began to rise. On the far side of the ballroom-sized structure was a pool of lava, glowing orange and creating an intense heat. Aylah raised her arms to protect her face from the hot fumes but continued forward. Suddenly the muddy ground beneath her gave way and she sank into the mud. She found no ledge around her to pull herself back up. She was slowly being engulfed in the mud and it began to burn and sting the deeper she sank. She could feel her toes blistering, letting out an involuntary scream as she continued to disappear into the torrid black maw.

Her scream echoed loudly in the chamber, and suddenly there was movement from the pool of lava. Out came the creature: the childlike black monstrosity pulled itself out of the liquid rock like it had been in a warm bath. It turned towards the sound of Aylah's scream, teeth flashing against the blazing lava light. It skittered towards her on all fours, although at this point in her agony Aylah couldn't comprehend anything but the pain she felt at being roasted alive. The creature grabbed her with a long tentacle-like appendage that protruded from under an arm, and pulled her out of the mud.

As she was dragged out, Aylah could tell most of her body had been badly burned, but the pain took a backseat to the fear she felt at seeing the creature again. It threw back its head, opening the tooth-filled mouth with an unhinged jaw, and made a screeching sound, a trumpet of elation, upon seeing her conscious. The sound sent cold fear deep into her bones. What was making this thing so happy?

Once it had dragged her completely out of the mud it gestured to her, pointing to her body with one of its three fingers. She was covered in giant leeches and her entire body felt on fire. They encased every inch of her body where she had sunk into the mud. All at once, like they felt her awareness, they opened their eyes. She was wearing a shroud of giant eyes, and they were all looking at her.

Before she could react, the creature howled: a loud shriek that startled the leeches. They detached from her body and dove back into the mud, eyes waving about wildly like they were in terrible pain. She lay there whimpering. Although the burning pain had dissipated upon the leeches releasing her, the psychological torment was still there, and her body was covered in dark, angry bruises. They might be gone but she could sense them out there, waiting for a chance to feed on her again.

She weakly raised her head. The thing stood above her, no more than three feet tall but towering over her in this weakened state. Sharp teeth still flashed malevolently. The small being was gesturing emphatically toward her, at something at the far end of the chamber. When she sat up, she saw it was pointing to two doorways. The creature made another gleeful sounding chitter at this revelation, and then scampered away on all fours, leaving her alone again.

Two doorways. The first quite obviously led down another corridor: muddy, dark, and foreboding, just like all the others in this underground maze. But the second... well that could not be. She stood up and hobbled painfully over to the second doorway, and instantly felt the cool breeze blowing

from it. The second doorway opened upon a dark forest trail. The kind that might be pleasant to take a hike on, late at night. As she stepped toward this doorway she did not hesitate. She needed to escape. There was no question in her mind which door to take... although at the last moment she felt one tug of discomfort, like some sort of déjà vu.

There was no way out. She'd been scraping at the dirt walls for hours to no avail, the hole was far too deep and the mud allowed her no grip to climb up the sides. She tried screaming but knew there was no one out in the woods this late at night to hear her, why had she decided to go hiking alone at this hour?

In the End
Joanna Dwyer

Have you ever been so crazy, fall-too-hard infatuated with someone that you wished you had never met them in the first place? You feel so silly, so naive, knowing how ridiculous and one-sided it is, but you can't stop it. You ache, get butterflies, and you wonder, even though you very well know it's all for naught. You just can't help but indulge and let your mind play around in fantasyland. You would rather lie in the belly of the beast of longing than get up and walk on.

When they met it was as if they were picking up where they had left off. Like it had already once been in motion. They existed in the night in dimly lit bars, quietly talking under the hum of conversation around them. As drinkers laughed and bullshitted about work and whatever happened to so and so, the two of them spoke so closely they could feel each other's words tickle their skin. They understood their language and conversed fearlessly; brazenly, daring the world to interject, and that was it.

Neither had any clue as to what had been set in motion; that what would ensue was inevitable and promised plenty of heartache, anger, frustration and, of course, a classic bittersweet ending.

The boy was the future main character. He had been

Photo by Daniel Dvorsky on Unsplash

here once before. Dark and slight with a devil's grin. He spoke lyrically, with slow deliberation, and preferred solitude to the company of useless minds and words. He kept his crazy to himself. Saved it for outlets that better understood. She thought this boy had slipped from her world chapters ago, but unfortunately here he stood again and she was helpless.

She had given up finding him and resigned herself to the fact that he would only exist in the pages she wrote and the songs she heard. Now, as she sat across from him, wondering how free she could be in front of him, the curtain closed and slowly reopened to reveal a familiar scene.

She lost the ability to control her words, her mind, her desire. She spoke in lyrics and confessed through riddles and songs. He made her breath catch every time he spoke words that cut right through her. He drew out the girl who had disappeared so long ago. She listened with disbelief as he proved himself to be exactly the one she thought had just been a memory .

Both parties very well knew that they were engaged in a fight that would be lost. Oh, how the complexities of life interfered relentlessly with the dos and don'ts, the shoulds and won'ts. They clung to their fantasyland in the cover of night, exchanging words and kisses, drinking every moment in, because they never knew when the sun would finally come to stay. One day the boy would be gone again and she'd keep him safely within the pages she wrote; ache for his words, his touch, and the way he would bounce one knee, lost in thought. All of this would eventually turn into a warm, dark, candlelit memory. Until then, she wouldn't take her eyes off him to be able to remember every detail of this moment in the long, dull and relentless stretch of living.

He would go on and she would pack it all in eventually, inevitably.

The worst of it was knowing all she would be left with was a heart full of 'what-ifs'.

They didn't mean to meet. In fact, their introduction was a good indicator that things were doomed from the start. She didn't just bump into him - she stumbled, tripped, and nose-dived full-force.

Oops.

They couldn't possibly stay away from one another. They gave no fucks about anyone else. Was it selfish? Absolutely, but was it wrong? That is a question the two of them never answered. It should have felt wrong. They should have been wracked with guilt. They should have acted like mature adults and stayed the hell away from each other. The problem was, no one opposed it. In fact, they were seen more as a couple than she and her fiancé were.

Her friends encouraged it. His friends loved it. The only person who would have been upset was clueless, lost in his own world of gratification.

It started with little excuses, but eventually they didn't even bother. It was easy. There was just enough sneaking to make it exciting, with such little resistance it felt natural.

She would wait for him in the cold, snowy nights of January, until he would sweep in quietly and keep Scarlett warm with the fire he lit deep within her. They sat in dim candlelight, sharing wine and talking, their conversations as natural and endless as the snow falling outside. She needed to feel hopeful, even just for a night; hope she could only find with him.

Time went so fast when they were together that she was always trying to make up for it. They shared an endless conversation via texting that paused when one fell asleep and resumed when they awoke the next day.

Scarlett had never experienced this. She'd had plenty of lovers, but never any love. Love was fleeting and pointless, phony and temporary. She'd felt love for her fiancé, once upon a time. It was exhilarating when they first met. He was exciting and dangerous and kept her guessing, always. In fact, she still wondered if he felt love for her. They shared no romance, no affection, and yet she stayed.

Why?

He had done her so much wrong over the years. He had repeatedly hurt her both intentionally and unintentionally. She had given up most of herself for him. The fact that he didn't deserve her was obvious. Scarlett had built him from the ground up, sacrificing and enduring for the sake of his happiness. What was the payoff for her? What kept her going?

Loyalty.

Despite their multiple trips to hell and back, despite the infidelity, the lack of romantic love, he was always and forever there. Scarlett never doubted that. They'd come so far together, battled the staunchest oppositions, doubts and naysayers just to prove everyone wrong. Their relationship was fueled by pride and the introduction of this new boy to Scarlett's life was a threat to that.

The clock was ticking and she would have to make the decision. Her heart wanted desperately to have a say in this, but her head was too strong. The fiancé was clueless and the boy refused to sway her one way or another. In fact, he kept his feelings completely to himself to avoid any ounce of bias. He was so stoic, Scarlett began to wonder if maybe their magic was all in her head.

She needed to hear the words from him. All he had to do was ask and she would jump freely. Though his actions made his feelings clear as day, he would not say it. Scarlett didn't hide a single thought, feeling or fantasy. She spoke openly about her desire to leave her fiancé for him. They often playfully fantasized about a life together, planning everything - their home, their wedding and everything else they could dream up. He drunkenly promised her all the things she wanted; all the things he wanted for her. He filled her up with hopes and dreams, stoking the mellow coals in her belly and making them burn.

But he just wouldn't do it. He wouldn't do the one thing she needed to make her choice - ask her to stay, to choose him. Some nights he would admit to a few feelings, the liquor holding his caution at bay. It was not enough, though. Scarlett couldn't convince herself that he loved her the way he made it seem. Was it all in her head? Was she totally fucked up? Was she imagining this entire thing? Their "love" was probably just alcohol-soaked loneliness, she would think.

But she couldn't deny that the laughter they shared was real, the tears they shed were real, the kissing was very real. People could see the chemistry between them. They had somehow become a couple to everyone but her fiancé. If he showed up at the bar without her, they asked where Scarlett was. They fit so naturally together that no one batted an eye when she took off with him at the end of the night. No one would sit in the seat next to him knowing that Scarlett would be there soon.

Everyone knew, but no one said a thing.

As the date of her departure grew closer, Scarlett's heart began to cry. She started convincing herself that it wasn't love. That loyalty was the better choice. Why should she trust this boy? She was naive to think that she was good enough for him and that the life she had imagined for them would become a reality. Fantasyland, as he called it. If she stayed, he would eventually see her for what she was. When the lights came on, when she took the makeup off, when she sunk into a depression or lost it in an anxiety attack, would he still want her then? What if he one day realized they should have been just an affair? What if it was all in her fucking head?

She couldn't risk it. Her heart was an idiot. Scarlett knew love was bullshit. Love was just a feeling. It wasn't something tangible. It wasn't a permanent state. Loving someone or being loved was irrelevant in the larger scheme of things. Love didn't guarantee a damn thing.

The predictability and stability of her "real" relationship was comforting, as she convinced herself more and more that the boy only saw her as a plaything, as entertainment, a muse. A body to keep him warm and lips for him to kiss. Scarlett was really just a distraction for him. At least, that's what she convinced herself of.

When she voiced these thoughts to him, he responded with outbursts of anger and frustration. He danced carefully around his own feelings and lectured her about her value as a person. He always told her she deserved so much more than she had, and when her fiancé came up in these heated conversations he got even angrier.

When Scarlett fished for compliments and reassurance, his passion tricked her into believing the love was mutual. He promised her the things she lacked, the things she desired deep down. She could hide nothing from him. He just knew. He knew what she wanted and needed; he could read the feelings in her eyes. Yet still she doubted it.

So, instead of softening, Scarlett slowly grew hard and cold. Vicious, even. She taunted him, ignoring him, ditching their usual nights together, showing up to the bar with friends instead. If she forced him away, it would justify her decision. But he knew exactly what she was doing and wouldn't play that game. His ability to shrug her behavior off drove Scarlett insane. Her temper flared, resulting in long, raging rants and name-calling.

Yet, he was still there. He waited patiently for her petulant behavior to subside as he knew it would. He knew her and he didn't want her to do anything she might regret.

He didn't want her to go. In fact, he couldn't get over the idea of never seeing her again. It made him angry and sad. It ignited a rage in him he'd long forgotten. He wanted to give her the world, but couldn't. The guilt of participating in an affair prevented him from telling the truth, from revealing the overwhelming adoration inside.

He just couldn't ask her to stay. He couldn't sway her decision. But he also couldn't get over Scarlett choosing the fiancé. Some nights when he'd overindulged at the bar, he'd start to slip up and express more of his feelings than he wanted. In her presence it took everything in him not to grab her and cry out and beg her not to do it. He didn't want her to leave. He wasn't sure he could bear it.

For some reason, since the night they met, he'd felt compelled to save her. He would leave her bottles of wine or packs of cigarettes outside her front door when he knew she was spending another night alone. As their relationship progressed, he began to offer her bigger, grander things in a desperate attempt to change her mind as she had changed his heart.

He'd sworn off love after a nasty split. He spent his life alone, working and developing an alcohol problem. He had a lot of money and spent it frivolously since he had no one to share it with. But all the booze he could consume and toys he could buy wouldn't fill the void inside.

Scarlett did.

Her presence warmed him. Her sarcasm and dry humor made him laugh. Her honest and true care for him was a shock. But her eyes were what stunned him the most. Deep blue and smiling, they sucked him in.

He knew she wanted him to ask. Scarlett was not discrete with her feelings and desires. Though she didn't know it, he had designed a life for them. He could see the dream house she'd described and imagined their life in it. Though he kept his own feelings locked down, some nights he let them out and let himself want her freely. On those nights, he'd send her evasive messages hinting that the love she brazenly admitted to was mutual.

But he absolutely would not ask her to stay. To choose him. He was a hypocrite and beat himself up for doing such terrible things with Scarlett. If he asked her to stay, he would be the bad guy, the homewrecker. Even though she could justify their actions, he couldn't. So if she stayed for him, the guilt would eat him alive. It had to come freely from her. It had to be 100% her choice without anyone else swaying her.

When she finally made her choice, he was devastated. He was hurt and pissed off. He'd truly believed she was going to choose him. Maybe all the love notes and confessions she'd made were a joke. A cruel game. Maybe it was all fake. The fantasyland she'd created was just that - a fantasy. This is exactly why he'd closed himself off - to avoid this entire mess.

Yet he couldn't let go of hope.

As she drove away from the city, from him, all she could see in her rearview mirror were her own tears. She screamed and gripped the steering wheel, exploding with live emotions. Passion and pain, rage and fear. She couldn't believe herself. She couldn't believe she was walking away, but she had come to realize that loyalty meant more to her than love. He

had become her only reason to stay and it wasn't that he wasn't enough, it's that everything else had become too much.

Less than twenty-four hours ago she was sitting in the passenger seat of his truck, parked on a lonely side street at midnight. There was a softness in his voice and Scarlett could hardly get two words out. Neither really knew what to say or how to do "goodbye". Their regular sarcastic banter and laughter were absent between kisses.

The lump in her throat was overtaking her, so she just sat back and stared stoically out the window in front of her. Looking at him was like taking a shot of whiskey. All the things she wanted to say burned her stomach. She wanted to grab him. Kiss him. Cry his name and tell him how far down the rabbit hole she'd really gone, but it was too late. It was too pointless. They both knew there was nothing left for them.

He had done more for her in one year than she could possibly express in that moment. The idea that this would be her last time with him was overwhelming. Unbearable.

Eventually he spoke. It was clear he had been organizing his thoughts for a while as his words were deliberate and honest. She half-listened, looking away when his eyes tried to meet hers. He went on about how much she'd meant to him, how much fun he'd had with her, how he'd enjoyed their endless conversations and mockery. A stream of memories flooded her brain, pushing the lump further up her throat. Tears dotted her eyes and she tried desperately to will them away as he went on. He was glad he could have been her "knight on a white horse," or whatever.

That one stung.

She hadn't thought about him like that, but she supposed it was true. When their paths crossed, Scarlett was a complete trainwreck in every possible way. She had tripped herself one too many times and forgotten how to get back up. She functioned on alcohol and cocaine and was quickly isolating herself as she tended to do when her self-loathing was winning. It was like she had been running toward a cliff, ready to jump, then he got in front of her, stopping her in her tracks with such force she couldn't see anything but him.

He didn't comprehend the gravity of his presence in her life. He wasn't a "white knight". He was a paramedic, saving her life on her journey to salvation. He'd given her everything she needed to breathe again, to walk again, to laugh again, to see that she could make it all by herself.

He finally finished his speech. He always made speeches, and she always smiled complacently at him, letting him go on to his heart's content before it was her turn to explode with sarcasm and clever remarks. But not this time. Now she reached out and put her hand on the back of his neck, her thumb briefly meeting his jaw.

They looked at one another exactly as they did the first time they sat in this very place. The first time he had kissed her. It had felt inevitable, that first one. They danced around it for hours, lingering, waiting for the other to make the move.

She was his. She'd slept with dozens of guys and kissed twice as many. But this one? It was her most brilliant memory. She'd replayed it in her mind the entire weekend afterwards like a teenager, smiling into the air for no good reason, biting her lip as butterflies floated around in her stomach. How could one kiss be so arousing and exciting?

Now, he kissed her like that again. Taking her head into his hands, his eyes focused on her lips. "Just one more kiss, right?" She nodded slightly, bracing herself. She wanted to burst with tears, but instead put all that energy into his mouth, kissing him as hard as she could. She wrapped herself around him and pulled them close together, but she couldn't get close enough. She grasped at him desperately, needing to feel his weight on top of her one more time.

They'd never had sex and she was glad of it. Everything they did was enough, always. But this? She could never get enough of it. His warm hands squeezing her hips, his chest pushed against hers, his warm mouth all over her face and neck. She

could hear herself breathing heavily as she ran her hands over him with urgency, trying to soak in every second before it was time to go. Her chest hurt from gulping down the lump that still clogged her throat. He stopped to look at her, her fiery hair now wound between his fingers. She was sure he could see her damp eyes and felt embarrassed.

In that moment, he could have said anything. Part of her wanted him to ask her to stay. He'd never asked her for anything though she was prepared to do just about anything. He opened his mouth and closed it again, looking away briefly. Scarlett ran her fingers through his jet-black hair and waited his moment out. Sadness flooded the truck, making it feel cold and empty. There was nothing left to say anyway.

He sat back in the driver's seat and chuckled. "You're gonna be fine, Scarlett." And she knew she would. She would be fine without him in her life, she just didn't want it that way.

They sat in silence which was heavy with words they both wanted to say but never would. It took Scarlett a while to compose herself enough to say goodbye. She leaned over and tenderly kissed him again, closed-mouth and slow, taking it in one last time.

Why the hell was she doing this? Why was she walking away from him? From this feeling? From his world?

But she had to. She said a quick, matter-of-fact goodbye and, with a dramatic sigh, let herself out of the truck and into the lonely night.

She was yanked from her pillow in a frantic, desperate jolt, reaching for air in her lungs. Her eyes searched the bedroom, confused and alone. Yes, she was alone though just moments ago he'd been there. They were talking as always, faces dancing closely, the magnet in him holding her tight and close. She swore his voice was just in her ear, but the empty room, hundreds of miles from him, said otherwise.

Fuck.

His warmth seeped out of her with a long, hopeless exhale. She fell back onto her pillow and the usual wave of sorrow consumed her body.

She hadn't touched him in two years. Hadn't felt his breath on her lips since that last night. She thought she'd made her peace and accepted her own damn choices; but some nights, she was brutally reminded that he no longer existed in her world.

Choking back a lump in her throat, Scarlett scanned through her sleepy phone, begging for some reminder that he was in fact there. They'd spent every night talking one another to sleep, then picking up where they left off in the early afternoon when the alcohol had been slept off. And it was new again. Every day. But now the night was only for her.

She'd thought she was over it all, but his melancholy had sucked her back in and her need to make sure he wasn't drinking with his demons went into overdrive. His sadness drove her insane and the thought of him alone with his mind scared her.

But he didn't need her. He didn't even want her to care anymore. She'd left. She'd chosen differently. But what he didn't know was the internal hell and turmoil she'd caused herself.

She wanted to scream for him. She wanted to get as deep into his arms as she could, his warm voice and familiar demeanor securing her safely from reality.

Nights were the loneliest without his words.

So she spent them aimlessly, wandering her quiet house in the dark, trying to count all the good things she had instead of taking inventory of all the things she'd lost when she left.

She'd wake up and fake it 'til she made it, and she was really fucking good at it.

But mornings like this threw her off and she was rendered useless, forced to grapple with her reality, and convince herself that he was just a dream. She just couldn't convince herself that she was better off.

That's all it would ever be. A dream. But now it was time to wake up.

The Legacy of Liberty Bell

Prologue to "The Truckstop at the Edge of the Universe"

Jeremy Morang

Space was empty, vast, dark, and cold.

For Liberty Bell, space was lonely and terrifying.

Her commandeered ship had finally stopped spinning after forty-five minutes of rolling and tumbling uncontrollably through the void. An overwhelming gravitational influence had gradually latched onto the port side of the craft and was dragging it. She wasn't expecting that. At least it stopped spinning, and the nausea stopped.

Sitting sideways in the co-pilot's chair with one boot propped up on a broken control stick, she rhythmically tapped the tip of a blood-crusted knife on her knee. The tablet resting in her lap was quickly losing power, and she attempted a smile whenever his image appeared. Tyreel's face vanished from the screen among momentary static, then rematerialized on the small monitor. Each time he came into view for a brief second, she stroked her thumb down his thick golden braids and wiped a tear from her cheek.

It was only a matter of time before he disappeared altogether, and she'd never see him again.

Knowing this unfortunate fact and swallowing down the tears, she unplugged the wires from the captain's dashboard, swung her legs to the floor, and approached the rear of the empty harvester. She was slow and careful not to touch her lodged sword on her way through the arch. Her dented, blood-stained blade was the one thing keeping her breathing. The only method of keeping the bay doors open was to use a tool large and thick enough to wedge into the framework and maintain air circulation throughout the ship.

She placed the tablet down on a table at the rear of the small craft, and then removed the backpack hanging from her shoulders. She dropped the black satchel beside Tyreel's flickering face and petted the frayed and tattered fabric with strokes of her dirty, grease-stained fingers.

Gripping the knife handle, she paced the storage room and searched the small enclosure for a means of escape, or any method of continued survival.

She muttered to herself while reaching behind a thin pipe along the ceiling, stretching for available power cables.

"If I can connect the oxygen reserve to the cockpit, close the doors and seal myself in," she said, thinking out loud, then paused, and her eyes followed the sound of invisible knuckles tapping along the floor below her feet. When the knocking on steel snaked away and vanished into the starboard hull, the butterflies in her stomach dwindled and she looked back to the wall.

"If I can conserve and reroute all the available power from back here, to the front… perhaps I can somehow divert the remaining energy from the scrubbers to the thrusters. It could work. It *has* to work." Gritting her teeth and digging for inner strength, she yanked the wires from a compartment overhead and the ship rocked to the side, knocking her to the floor.

"Damn it!" she yelled at the wall, "Give me something to work with here!" The corners of her mouth turned down and she pointed to the open compartment. "Now, listen up. You take care of me and I'll be sure to take care of you. We have a deal?" The tapping knuckles returned, and climbed the port side wall. "I'm sorry I did this to you. Just relax for a second, please? Let's talk this through." The tapping stopped and the familiar *groan* echoed around the bay. "My crew will have you fixed up and looking pretty again in no time. Just get me back to the Truckstop, and everything will be fine. I promise. Just get me home."

In response, the starboard side of the craft rattled behind her.

"Not much time. Not much time." She scrambled to her feet and tore off her long jacket. Behind her pointed ears and across her neck, beads of sweat formed and crawled down her skin to the collar of her dark shirt. With a side arm-toss, the blood-stained coat was thrown to the wall, and rolling up her sleeves, she quickly returned to the cockpit to try something different.

The dashboard lights flickered and dimmed when she attempted a power transfer switch underneath the frame. The small craft lurched to the side and returned her to the co-pilot's chair in a crumpled heap. The damaged thruster sputtered, then died, and the toolbox secured to the pilot's seat loosened from its mount. It slid across the floor and clattered by her feet into the cargo bay. On its way over the grated threshold, the corner of the heavy black metal box struck the handle of her sword. The blade came free and the doors slowly closed.

"No!" She screamed and dashed to the rear, sliding sideways between the thick steel before it slammed shut. The edge of the door clipped her foot, and she was sprawled out flat on her back.

Lying motionless on the floor, she stared at the thin crossbeams above her.

"*Fuck*," she whispered, and placed both palms over her eyes.

After a moment of silence, and contemplating what might happen if she didn't find a way out of this mess, she clenched both fists and screamed at the ceiling.

"FUCK!"

I can't do anything.

Her wide eyes darted to each corner.

There's no way out of this. There has to be a way out. I didn't come all this way…

Absentmindedly, the small blade twirled around her fingers and she looked to its blood-crusted edge. "There is way out. There's always a way. Listen to your own advice, Liberty." A final dark solution slithered into her thoughts.

She was finally defeated, after the hours of seemingly endless torture. Aching and sore, bruised, and beaten. Her battered body and clothes were tattered and slashed. Half an ear was missing and she rubbed her fingers over four crescent moons carved in her throbbing forehead. Her sweat dampened and blood crusted hair was stuck to her cheek and throat. Exhausted, and ready, she sat on the floor beside the table and rested her head against the warm steel.

At least it'll all be over. At least I'll win.

I told him I'd win.

After a moment of pondering, staring, and recalling the events that led her to the choice of ending the pain quickly, his ominous, intrusive voice drifted into her memories.

Don't let your legacy end this way. Choose life. Choose to live, Liberty. Follow your destiny. The path to bliss.

"I told you: I'd rather die." She wiped the last of her tears away with the back of her hand.

Eyes pressed closed, she turned her face to the ceiling. She swallowed hard, concluded there was no other way, and placed the sharp steel on her wrist.

The dried blood of the enemy meshed into her flesh, but she couldn't apply enough pressure to draw blood of her own. Her hand shook, and with each nervous twitch, the knife was pulled away with a quick jerk.

She'd hold her breath, try to relax, and attempt again.

With each effort, the blade pushed further and deeper toward the veins. It would go in eventually. The moment she felt as if it may finally slice through, a small spot of warm blood finally welling to the surface, she half smiled. Serenity would soon be on its way to find her.

Her eyes opened when a bolt from a crossbeam fired down from overhead striking the steel beside her foot.

She pulled the knife away and fought another wave of tears.

"No, no. Not this. I can't go out like that."

Taking it as a sign, she leaned forward and stood on shaking legs.

Hoping she had enough power remaining for one more search, she grabbed the tablet from the counter and pressed the screen. She accessed the harvester interface and ran a quick secondary scan of the ship's structure. Desperate to know how much estimated time she had left on the clock, and what her remaining options entailed.

Her finger scrolled through the available information. "Unlimited air, that's good. No food or water. Not good. No weapons. Still no navigation. Systems are completely fried. External heat index and pressure indicator shows a full structural collapse in possibly three hours, give or take. Three hours." She stopped and cautiously glanced to the knife on the table. She looked back to the tablet. "Thrusters, useless. Ship to ship communications, destroyed. What's this?"

She quickly accessed the harvester's internal functions display and a light flashed on the screen. After she managed a quick glimpse, the tablet flashed a white glow and then died.

"A locator beacon." She looked up from the darkened screen and whispered. "I can rig the damaged array, to transmit a locator beacon. Why not? It *could* work." She raised her hands to her hips and looked to the floor between her feet. "Certainly worth a try. A location buoy. Rig the array to transmit my voice, and hope for the best. And I have three hours to pull it off." She nodded slowly and moved her focus around the ship to each panel and available control box along the four walls surrounding her.

At the stern of the harvester she followed a conduit to a small door recessed in the wall behind a crew member's empty bunk. Using the knife tip, she pried open the door and looked inside. The panel housed a congestion of thick wires and computer components which ran up and down within the framework and spread through the hull.

Before she made the first of the wire cuts, a soft voice spoke behind her. An unwelcome whisper she had become acquainted with over the course of the day had crept back into her ears. Down on one knee, she peeked over her shoulder to the backpack on the opposite side of the cargo room, which was taunting her from afar.

Liberty, the most powerful tool in the universe is in there. Use it. At least then, you'll know how to better prepare.

"No." She replied. "I know how this all ends. I have two options, don't I?" She sliced through a thick wire and stripped the coating away. "It's always two options, right? Either, someone finds me and takes me home, or I'll be cooked to a crisp." She pried a circuit board from the housing and snipped a wire from a control chip. "I might get crushed to death, and then cooked, or cooked then

crushed, doesn't matter. But either way it all goes down, I still win. I beat you. You better remember that, asshole."

The knife edge twisted the head of a screw and as she applied pressure, the blade slipped and tore through the tip of her finger. The slice ripped half her pinky nail free and exposed the bone inside the meat. She dropped the blade and backed away from the wires, holding the wound under her armpit. The voice beckoned a second time.

All you had to do was listen and you wouldn't be in this mess.

Using her teeth, the blood soaked tourniquet around her upper arm was untied and then quickly wrapped around the wounded finger. She hissed at the wall, "No. No surrender. I serve no master."

The whispering air swirled and glided to each corner. Liberty followed it with her eyes around the small room.

You always choose the difficult path, Intendant Bell. Why don't you ever take the easy route? If only you had followed your path. The right path. Your cosmic destiny.

She spoke to the space above her: "I choose the right path. I'll always choose the right path. I'm doing what I need to do, so we all survive this. I don't care about you! You're nothing to me. All I care about is the Exterior. You keep telling me to keep my legacy alive." She tapped her chest, taking ownership of her decisions, and then pointed to the satchel. "I leave my legacy of my own accord. You don't dictate my destiny, I do! This is my legacy! This is what I choose! This is what I was meant to do!" She strode across the floor and waggled her finger at the table. "Don't ever tell me about my fate. My fate is in my hands. You say you make the rules, and I say I'm changing them this time around! Bet you didn't see that shit coming, did you?! Pack it up and go home. You lost, admit it."

She looked away from the bag. "Now, leave me alone! I have something to do." She returned to the panel, pulled her hair behind her ears and reached into the hull.

The disembodied voice hovered over her shoulder. *Liberty, you may not know it yet, but it may make all the difference. I'm sure you understand that. Don't allow your stubborn nature to discount all the possible options. You may be surprised by what you experience. That's it. Come on over. Just one more and then you can do whatever it is you need to do. I promise to leave you alone. A little closer.*

Transfixed and hypnotized by its power, approaching the table with her arm outstretched, she untied the bag flap and opened it wide. Fighting the influence and the echoing voice in her mind, she reached inside the backpack and held her hand above the most powerful weapon ever created. A device once thought to be nothing more than an ancient myth. A myth told to children. The draw was magnetic. She could feel her skin wanting to make contact and as her fingers moved ever closer, her breathing hitched and her heart pounded out of control against her chest bones.

Just one more inch, Liberty. Then you will have what it is you truly seek.

Remembering what happened the last time she connected, she snapped out of the trance and said: "No." She withdrew her hand and stepped back. "I'm all done with you. This is where the game ends."

I understand. I'll be here when you need me.

She spun from the bag and returned to her duties.

The backpack remained silent as she devoted the next twenty minutes to rigging the harvester's array network. She cut wires and cables, spliced together and reconnected circuits and power components. All the panels and control boxes were pried open or removed from their hinges. Direct ship-to-ship communications were obsolete, but a locator beacon would provide decodable coordinates for a Trucker, or a passerby in proximity, if they ever discovered the signal while flying through the sector. The risk being, she had three hours to be found, in a vast empty wasteland, while being dragged to a violent death.

The odds were never in her favor.

She determined the beacon was her only viable option. She could sit in an empty steel space, alone, and wait to die horribly. Or, slide the blade through the flesh and end it quickly, ending her legacy forever. Or, make use of the only equipment at her disposal to try something different.

Sometimes a third option presents itself when least expected.

Connecting the final wire into the device and tightening it to the casing with a clamp found in the toolbox, she utilized her tablet as a makeshift transfer conduit to complete the task. She finished her newly designed array, and the end result was a series of multicolored wires crisscrossing above her, and snaking out across the floor and three of the walls. She stepped back from her spiderweb wire creation at the center of the bay and pressed the rigged tablet screen to test its functionality.

On the blue display where Tyrcel's face used to be, the beacon activated with a bright, blinking red light. Awestruck and speechless that it actually worked, she dropped to her knees before the mechanism and sobbed into her palms.

She wept. A silent cry. No sounds, only tears. The only noises uttered were when she drew in another deep breath to continue her bawling and purging it from her system. When a dribble of drool ran down her bottom lip, she tucked her chin to her chest and her shaking arms wrapped tight around the torso.

She inhaled through her nose and forced the tears to stop. *I have to keep it hidden. Keep it buried with all the other secrets.* She released the white knuckle embrace she had on her body, lifted her head slowly, and laughed at the ceiling. Belly chuckling replaced the sadness as she returned to the floor flat on her back and crossed one leg over the other. Tears formed at the corners and she swiped them away with a thumb. Pleased with the new paradigm, her eyes locked with the computerized spider web suspended before her and she said, "Always take the third option, right Tyreel?"

The red light blinked its response and urged her to begin. It was only a matter of time before all power was gone and the beacon would terminate. No time to get cocky and arrogant. After the power was drained, she'd be forced to again choose from the two original options. Wait and die violently by natural forces, or end it all.

If it came to death by her own hand, she'd use the blade that initially started the journey. A journey that began over thirty years earlier.

It was time to get busy. Time to send the message before it was too late.

She tapped the screen and the recording application appeared on the monitor. "Test, test," she whispered to gauge its recording strength.

Her faint voice transformed to written data and the tablet recorded the two words. After she paused and waited for the response, the array projected the test words into the void.

"Son of a bitch, will you look at that."

She programmed the device for three hours of recording time, methodically calculated her spatial location into the system, and pressed the transmit button. Now all that was left to do was wait and hope.

And tell her story to anyone who might be listening.

Rolling the jacket into a ball, she placed it beneath the hanging monitor and dropped the back of her head into the blood-crusted fabric. She fluffed up the sides to make a comfortable cushion and once she found her spot of comfort on the grated floor, she laced her fingers over her stomach and sighed.

"Here we go."

During the momentary pause of gathering her thoughts and organizing her memories, the recorder sent the short message away from the ship, into the blackness of space.

She breathed deep and started her speech. "This is High Intendant Liberty Bell. Owner and operator of Truckstop One, in Sector One of the Vega Grid. Exterior Deep I.D. credentials: Titan, two, two, four, zero, four. Kallarian issued bounty hunting license verification is: Red Hall, valor, lavender, nine. Confirmation with Elder Collector, Sid. Personal Retriever Runner, active pilot code, Titan eight, eight, seven. My spatial grid coordinates are zero, zero, three, Alpha, and there's a good chance by the time you get here, I'll be long dead or vanished from radar forever. If this message can somehow reach the Omega Gate, it may find someone with an open channel who can assist me, but I have to consider this may never happen. My message will reach someone someday. That's what's most important. I have to believe that. Everyone needs to know what happened today and the events that brought me here and why I'm doing what I'm doing to save everyone I can. Please get this message out to all citizens of the Exterior. At this point, my best-case scenario is, you'll find me quickly and I can continue my mission."

The ship rumbled and vibrated, and the backpack whispered, *this is a colossal waste of time, Liberty.*

She ignored the voice and maintained her focus on a crossbeam.

"I encountered the Lishoku Del'Amma earlier today and was provided a choice. I didn't like the options and responded in a manner they found unsuitable. I can't be sure if they're listening, or will ever find this message, but if you're out there and you can hear me you miserable bastard: fuck you!"

The glass in the cockpit shattered on the opposite side of the sealed door and the steel bowed around the framework from the pressure change. She lurched to her feet and stared the door down and waited for the buckling steel to implode and finish it all. She closed her eyes and clenched her fists and waited for the air to be sucked from the room.

The ship quieted again and her eyes fluttered open.

She relaxed her breathing and hesitantly returned to the pillow. She looked away from the doors and continued the recording.

"The only way to save the Exterior, the colonies, and the remaining survivors scattered throughout the cosmos, was to get it as far away as possible. That's the only way. No other choice. Unfortunately, for me, I'm the only one qualified enough to see it through to the end." Her hands covered her eyes and she sighed. "We come as a package deal and I still wish I knew why. I wouldn't be recording this and speaking to a faceless audience, if I had any other options. I was almost there. I was so close. I had the coordinates locked in and only one jump remaining. I failed, and now I'm here. I may be close to my end. I may not survive this, but I'm taking the prize with me to my death." She glanced to the satchel and tore her eyes away quickly so as not to get distracted.

"If I can pull this off, I might just save the universe and everyone in it. Any local, long-range Truckers along shipping lanes one and two who might be scavenging the Milky Way or any harvester pilots in proximity to my location, if you can hear me, I'm on a slow collision course with Earth's sun. I have an estimated three hours before I'm crushed to death or cooked to a crisp and if you find me alive and well and assist me in what I need to do, you'll become rich beyond your wildest dreams. You just need to locate my position. Please hurry."

She wiped a watering eye and sniffled. A wave of sudden emotions swallowed her in sadness as she came to grips with her reality. When her lips stopped trembling she continued, "This is my full open confession to the authorities and to all the Directors at Jericho City who may be free from the enemy's influence, and in accordance with Narroo customs and practices, this is also my official last will and testament. Unfortunately, I don't have a face-to-face witness right now, so you'll have to suffice." Butterflies erupted in the bottom of her stomach, and she dry heaved. "I need someone to talk to and you're all I have left in the universe. I've come to believe my impending death, or my hopeful surviv-al, serves the greatest purpose in history. I will win this. I know I will. There's no other choice. I have to win. If I'm unable to complete my original mission, the surface of a sun is a good secondary plan." She reached to her throat where the master key used to hang. Remembering she no longer possessed it, her hands returned to the floor.

"No matter what, the enemy cannot complete their goals. My legacy, my reason for being, my purpose, is to ensure they fail, regardless of what they told me or what they promised. In order for this to work, I have to tell my story, and as long as I continue speaking, the locator will continue to trans-mit. My voice will leave a trail of crumbs to follow, and anyone who stumbles upon the signal in your travels, you'll be able to decode the transmission and triangulate my location." Her voice quivered and she stuttered over her words and to gain control, she had to swallow each lump rising in her parched throat.

"If you're unable to locate me, please get my message, or whatever was recorded of this message, to Jericho City as soon as possible. This is all I have left. I am officially out of options. Now, knowing my rigged invention actually worked, and I still have three hours before I'm burnt to a crisp in this tin can, I'm going to step away for a minute or two and have one more cry. When I'm done getting it out of my system once and for all, I'll record, and begin transmitting again. I won't be gone long."

TRANSMISSION PAUSED

Copyright © 12/19/18, Jeremy Morang

Photo by Toa Heftiba on Unsplash

Ravenous
Hannah Ifeoluwa

Why have you come, you ravenous beast?
You feed on our flesh, you tear our guts
We are your preys, the monster we fear
You strip us of our pride
You snatch our dignity from us
We run to those who say they hunt you
Only to know they nurse you
You have made our mothers weep all day
Our fathers bite their fingers in dismay
Your howls have come to steal our sleeps
Why have you come, you ravenous demon?
You ignore the dried tears on our cheeks
You turn deaf ears to the cries of young ones
Waylaying them on the way to the future
Our blood quenches your thirst
In those eyes, we see pure evil flames
Those claws have made marks unforgotten
Long fangs bringing along nightmares
Why have you come, you ravenous destroyer?
I wish we all live to see your end
But to face you, we all abscond
Endless fear pushes us against walls
With painful heart, we have embraced you to stay

The Doe
Randy Thompson

Sunlight streams through tree tops
The forest floor is speckled with its brilliance
A gentle stream slowly moves fallen birch leaves along on their journey
Beside an ancient oak stands the doe
She is watchful, she is vigilant, she is not afraid

The doe lifts her head and smells the breeze
The morning has called her to the stream to drink
Her sisters are in the distance, she is aware of each one
A single sprig of clover across the stream catches her eye
She is watchful, she is vigilant, she is not afraid

The doe stretches forward to sniff the morsel
A squirrel in the distance is vexed
The doe lifts her long neck and listens, she is stillness itself
A willow twig crackles with warning
She is watchful, she is vigilant, she is not afraid

BANG !..........   BANG!........
The forest echoes with offence as loud as river ice breaking in deepest winter
The smell of sulphur is on the wind, it is foreign to the forest but known to all in its
keep
The doe is primed with purpose
She is watchful, she is vigilant, she is not afraid

BANG! .... comes the third
The doe feels its percussion across the hairs of her flank
Fly away! Fly away! Fly away!
Muscles surge in unison, she is lightning itself
She is watchful, she is vigilant, she is not afraid

The forest opens before her
She is swift as the hawk swoops, she is light, she is wind
Hooves dig into frost-covered moss, her heart pounds in her chest
The spruce and hemlock entreat her – come!
She is watchful, she is vigilant, she is not afraid

The doe knows that she need not run too far
It is not the wolf or the coyote which hunts her
Her senses are at their highest, her blood is hot with excitement

Escape is her promise and she is faithful to it
She is watchful, she is vigilant, she is not afraid

On a sunny knoll, she stops
Her sisters are in the distance, she is aware of each one
Her ears probe the expanse, she hears only the chewing of a fat porcupine
She shakes the perspiration from her coat and snorts loudly
She is watchful, she is vigilant, she is not afraid

Sunlight streams through tree tops
The forest floor is speckled with its brilliance
A gentle stream slowly moves fallen birch leaves along on their journey
Beside an ancient oak stands the doe
She is watchful, she is vigilant, she is not afraid

A selected poem from The Water Logs
KMJVB

Lips locked and loved.
Life.
Languid longing unleashed.
Seaweed sex and subjugation,
Fusion.
Stars above and so below,
I love you more than you know.
Breath and bubbles shared,
Eternity is ours with the surface break,
And first gasps taken together....
You,
I'd share air with you....
My ever-beloved aqualung.

Unseeded
Tissy Taylor

Legs splayed wide open
Hazy and broken
Can't figure it out
Cold steel pressing you
Want, to pull you out
Refuse discarded
No chance to begin
Never would you win
No voice
No choice
Decision is made
Nothing is fated
A seed without hope
A child with no voice
Placards spell dismay
Young girl, head bowed she
Is tired and worn
Share your crazy rants
Poor and all alone
Who decides
What is right

Filthy commoner
Bloody, stupid whore
This child
Respite
God smite
Her existence
Is unmoral
Still this life she gives
A decision lived
Wondering what if
This seed if it lived
If she did believe
On your wedding day
My darling I pray
The girl I see now
The one I let go
I will never know
Who you would become
I made a choice
To end your life
Before it was
And haunting me
Always will be
What you could have been

Cathartic Circle
Eddie Eichelberger

It's been 3:59 for about five hours now.

I'm sure I'll hear that somebody wrote something similar to that at some point in time, but for now I'm claiming *cryptomnesia*—something I just learned about this morning. If you're bored at work like I am right now, you can google that.

I'm in a hurry for four o'clock, because then I'll only have one hour left.

When I interviewed for this job, I told the interviewer that were I to get the position, this would literally be the nicest place I've ever worked! It was a brand-new, beautifully designed building that has a café, gym, multiple game rooms, and walls painted with alternating primary colors. When they offered me the position, I jumped at it! Over time, however, I grew to hate this place, and now I can't wait to get out. And there are more than enough cascading windows flanked by potted palms letting in glorious sunlight that could afford me a very memorable departure.

As aesthetically pleasing as this place is, it also happens to be the least friendly place I've ever worked. I *would* say the people I work with hate me, but I'm pretty sure they don't feel anything that strongly. It's been said the opposite of love isn't hate but indifference, and there's nobody on my team I could point to and comfortably say they would piss on me if I were on fire.

I've worked a lot of places over the years, and I've never had a problem making friends. Sure, I've had "personality conflicts" with one or two people before, but never *all* the people I've had to work with. Don't get me wrong. They're polite and helpful and all, but the fake plastic smiles plastered on their well-meaning faces every time we unavoidably walk past each other is enough to make me want to ask what the fuck I ever did to make them not like me in the first place. However, that would give them the satisfaction of knowing that I care why they don't like me. And that's assuming they would care that I care that they don't like me, which I doubt…

When I first came to work here, I would try to jump in on my team's high-spirited conversations. *"I love that movie! My car does the same thing! Oh, my God, have you ever tried their coconut shrimp?"* Whenever I did that all the air would go out of the discussion and they'd just go back to work.

I sometimes wonder if it's because I'm a temp. Did I mention I was a temp? I'm older than all but one of them (the manager) and I wonder if they don't like me because I'm a reminder that there's no such thing as job security and they may be temps themselves one day.

God, that would be sweet!

I know it's not because I'm an outsider. Other outsiders—vendor representatives that don't technically work for the company, but for some reason come to work here every day and sit in our desk clumps—come and go through our group and they're embraced by the team.

Maybe it's because I'm a dude. It's a group of six people (five employees and one outsider) and only two of the six are other guys. One is the manager, so it's not like they're going to not like him. And, to be fair, the manager is the one person in the group that does check in with me to see how I'm doing. I was right when I said he wouldn't piss on me if I were on fire. That dude would throw a blanket over me and roll me around until the fire's out, then help me up again and brush me off!

The other guy on the team is a muscularly chiseled, charismatic Asian guy and everybody just thinks he's the bee's knees! Aside from the manager, he's the only other person that is even remotely friendly, but it's not exactly a bar that's been set very high. He'll talk to me to when it's just the two of us running an errand or something so it's not awkward, but lately he just walks up to my desk, spits out parameters for whatever report he wants me to run as I furiously write them down, and then walks off to put water in his goddamn pretentious coffee press.

You couldn't put that in an email?

I wonder if it's because I don't go into their meetings with them. I guess I'm not privy to whatever the hell they're discussing in there that's so terribly secret. Between you and me, I'm glad I don't have to go into those meetings. I can hear them through the closed door of the adjacent conference room just cracking each other up.

Three months ago, there was a big shuffling around of people in the office to streamline the groups we all sit in. I was the only one on my team that was moved away from the team. And this is how I know I'm not the problem. The new group I was moved next to started talking to me. They actually engaged me in conversation!

Holy shit, it's 4:36!

Not long after the move, we had a "Spring Marketing Event". This was a luncheon that was set up in one of the big presentation rooms downstairs. My team was finishing up one of their "everybody but me" meetings right before it started, so I got down to the party before the rest of them. I sat at a big, empty table all by myself and made a bet with myself that my team wouldn't sit with me. And, sure enough, one by one, every single person on my team walked right past me and sat at the next table where I had a great view of them eating and cracking each other up.

The people on the other team I had been moved next to watched it all happen. Finally, one of them said to me, "Eddie, why don't you sit with your table?"

"They don't want to sit with me!" I replied indignantly, trying not to sound like the smelly kid at school.

"Not your team", said the nice lady. "Your *table*!" That's what we call our desk clumps. Trying not to look too elated, I picked up my plate and went over to join them. And they actually engaged me in conversation!

As nice as my new neighbors are, however, I'm not on their team so there are times when they're off doing their own thing and I'll be all by myself in the desk clump. This place has given me the unique opportunity of knowing what it feels like to be the center section of a Venn diagram. There are many circles I interact with, but I don't have a circle of my own.

I have this fantasy where I quit without notice and print out an "open letter" to the company I thought would be an awesome place to work. I thank the handful of people that were friendly to me and tell the rest of them they can all kiss my ass in Hell. Then I'd clip the letter to my monitor with the badge I need to get into this place, but I also need that badge to get out of this place, so that would be difficult.

So what am I doing to get out of here? Admittedly, not as much as I should. I've always been a "bird in the hand" kind of guy. If I have a job, why should I worry about finding another job. And then there's the fact that I'm just lazy, but I still manage to send out the occasional application and resume. Another saying goes, "we are the cause of our own suffering", and I'm definitely guilty of that! Or as my old man used to say: "Some people just aren't happy unless they have something to bitch about!"

It seems like just a couple minutes ago it was 3:59, but it's been 4:59 for about five hours now. Figure *that* shit out!

An Ode to the Alphabet
M.E. Shao

The Letter "A"

A picture says a thousand words
At least that's what they say
Although they can't describe a thing
As well as the letter "A"

"A" means that there's others
As if there's two or three
And if there was just only one
"A" would become "the"

The Letter "B"

Behold! A letter that can be
Better than numbers one and three
Because it sits quite neighborly
Between its buddies A & C

Boldly standing faithfully
Barely used the same you see
Bugs will spell it differently
But one less E and then it's be

The Letter "C"

Can you guess what letters next
Clocking in at number three?
Careful how you use it now
'Cause it confuses frequently

Certain times it's overlooked, like
Chief – the "I" before the "E"
Can't use "I" that same way though
Coming after "C"

The Letter "D"

Dare I try letter four
Daunting as it may be?
Duly note this verse might prove
Drab and dull as me

Don't say there's other letters of such
Deep complexity
Desire to speak in a past tense?
Dread not! Just add a "D"

The Letter "E"

Ere I forget I said I'd commit
Ever mindful I shall be, and
Execute my promise, my Oath
Elegantly thanking thee

Eyes see so much wisdom
Ears hear so much glee
Every single word of love
Ends, with letter "E"

The Letter "F"

Finally a letter without a long E
For those are easy to rhyme
Frankly it's fun to come up with a pun
Fresh from out of the mind

Forever I wonder, over and under
From bottom to top, all the time
For a bold new way to come out and say
F this…but with no moral fine

The Letter "G"

Goodness gracious, golly G!
Gifted writers inspire me
Gernsback, Goddard, de Graffigny
Grouped in glory's category

Guiding words with paper and pen
Grandeur achieved by all of them
God bestowed them minds of gold
Goals to emulate when I'm old

The Letter "H"

Heavens hopeful, but all should know
Hell awaits for heathens below
Havoc, hatred, halls of stones
Heated seats on hopeless thrones

Helping mortals foster love
Hoping for the gates above
Hearts are kind for constant fear
Horror and nightmare might be near

The Letter "I"

I love the vowels for how they serve
In bridging letters, creating words
Insanity comes, 'cause if not for them
Illegible messes none comprehend

Idle time attempting to read
It's pointless were it not for these
Irked by consonants, throw in the towel
If you want a word…just buy a vowel

The Letter "J"

Jack and Jill went up the hill
Jogging straight up and down
Joking and playing, having a thrill
Joy till he broke his crown

Jumping in fear, Jill looked around
Jolting across the way
Jeering, she returned and scooped him up
Jill's stick was shaped like a J

The Letter "K"

Knobbed in darkness, twisted wood
Knuckled as can be
Kinks and dead spots all around
Knotted is the tree

Kindling yes, our God will need, as its
Key for making day
Kind, He brightens nights with
Knights, by simply adding K

The Letter "L"

Little, little, did I know
L is oh so great
Like the time I drank that wine and
Lulled a pretty mate

Lords and ladies, boys and girls
Like all, must pay the well
Lay respect to that which lets us
Love – the letter "L"

The Letter "M"

Middle of the alphabet
Molded like a gem
Most will say there's nothing worth
More than Letter "M"

Maybe M hates W
Malice with a frown
Mercilessly mocked by him when
M is upside down

The Letter "N"

Naughty naughty little N
Never helping me
Nothing useful ever comes from
Negativity

No and never, none and nor
N is oh so rude
Neighbors M and O must want to
Nix that attitude

The Letter "O"

Over, under, bottom, top
Odes to letters never stop
On the day I get to Z
Old and wrinkled, I may be

Or young and youthful, hopefully
Only time will tell, you see
Our lives are short, we need to grind
Otherwise we're wasting time

The Letter "P"

Paper, pencil, pen and ink, in
Prose I've grown to speak and think
Public platforms, message boards
Poetic guide of rhythmic chords

Poems are pretty, I think it naught
Pretentious such as some have thought
Pious I shan't think it so
Poetry shall help me grow

The Letter "Q"

Quiet! I must concentrate
Q is hard to satiate
Quarrels make me want to quit
Quirks in words which don't quite fit

Quorum comes when all are here
Quickly now, our quest is near
Quantify a love for two
Q is married, to the U

The Letter "R"

Regal existence, loved from afar
Reality dictates we need Letter R
Rigid and rugged it's straight and it's curved
Reading is easy when Rs are preserved

Rallying troops or driving a car?
Really won't work without Letter R
Reason without one, your point is moot
R runs the game, expect the boot

The Letter "S"

Supposed vision we are told will
Save the world today
Sorry if I disagree
So many told to stay

Spite and harm are currently
Sawing through the way
Someday hope for peace and love
So hate will go away

The Letter "T"

There never was a letter
That can do as much as me
Think about it really hard and
Thank me when you see

The other letters hate me
Though, because of jealousy
They say it's not fair that I rhyme
That super easily

The Letter "U"

Usually I'd try her number
Unfortunately my hearts asunder
Used to love her, used to hold
Useless now, attempts are cold

Until things change for now I'll be
Under this cloak of melancholy
Urging progress, longing for more
Unable to close the heart wrenching door

The Letter "V"

Very strong, vivaciously
Voltage high, tenaciously
Veer this verse, voraciously
Vaulting over prose you see

Violence in these words you read
Viking frame of mind have we
Vibrant in philosophy
Verbiage is our currency

The Letter "W"
Well, here we are
Woe is me!
Winding down, finally
Wrapping up this poetry

We're almost done, from A to Z
Writing alphabetically
Won't be long, but wait! We're not free
W was easy….X will not be

The Letter "X"
X can mark the spot I see
Xanax needed this entry
Xi is Greek, it's fourteen
Xeroxed words, all randomly

Xystus too, as I mentioned Greece
Xebecs sailing open seas
Xerosis I suffer cerebrally
Xenial X was not to me

The Letter "Y"
You may think these odes of mine
Yawn-inducing, wastes of time
Yet I attest validity
Yes they're written passionately

Yesterday I couldn't show it
Younger me was not a poet
Yearn for greatness, one day bestow it
Years from now, I hope you know it

The Letter "Z"
Zealots desired to bless my soul
Zilch is my energy left
Zoned out, these odes have taken their toll
Zoo in my mind, though 'twas deft

Zip up this project, my brain can now rest
Zero letters now lie ahead
Zephyrs now soothe me, caressing my chest
Zodiac today – time for bed

Choices
Jai Thoolen

When she first found she was pregnant,
Her whole world was torn apart.
Her mind was doing back-flips,
And those thoughts destroyed her heart.

That night kept playing over,
On repeat inside her mind.
He was ruthless. He was vicious.
It was rape of the worst kind.

There were threats and there was violence.
There was blood, bruises and tears.
Those visions never fading,
And she'd live them all her years.

Her hardest life decision.
Should she keep a rapist's kid?
Impassioned moral choices,
And in the end, she did!

Her eyes first saw this baby,
And then horror flooded in.
A love like this must rally,
Because all she saw was HIM!

Puke Reverence
Ayo Gutierrez

Holy Bible
Hundred-dollar bills
High heels

You summon the windows of heaven
to pour down its blessings
on these lovely maidens
in their white robes and high heels
who open their purse and wallets
and shout Amen!
while they willingly
part their legs for you
to receive your good omen
and their old folks
filling your stomach
with the finest fattening

a fitting arrangement
you told me
for them
to gain salvation

I never questioned a man of God.

You are one nebulous specter
of a charismatic leader
gaining momentum in
this rollicking ride
of madness contagion
a beast put in a leash
under the cloak of modesty
And I've seen this beast
freed
a hundred times
its insatiable appetite
salivating
feeding
on youthfulness
and innocence...

But I would never question a man of God.

Tonight
we say our prayers together
and I drink in your sermon
in my white robes and high heels
your simple fetishes:
this Holy Bible
hundred-dollar bills
and high heels
I say in one breath
in an upbeat march
as I cut you in three pieces
for desecrating
Cristina, Olivia, and Sarah
our dearest daughters

No need for a tomb and a grave
these effigies will burn
with you
the smoke and the fire
very much alive
celebrating your demise
while I break free
from your grasp
no longer the
spiritless slave to your caprice

I am the new God.

Noises in the Night
Corrie Lavina Knight

An eerie noise crawled up from the basement and settled between my shoulder blades, raising the hair on the back of my neck. "It's just the furnace," I assured myself. Pausing from knitting to rub my aching fingers, I glanced out the picture window to see darkness outside—when did that happen?

Tap. Tap-tap. Tap.

The bush I forgot to prune last summer played in staccato on the quarter-pane window in the corner, telling me the wind was picking up a little. I stood and crossed the room to adjust the thermostat, then shrugged into my trusty cable knit sweater. Shivering, I went into the kitchen and flipped the switch on the electric kettle. A situation like this could only be remedied with a peanut butter sandwich, a bowl of soup and a mug of hot cocoa.

As I rummaged in the cupboard for the can of Campbell's I could have sworn was in here a few days ago, I heard the back door to the garage swing open, then slam shut. Not again. Dread wrapped icy tentacles around my stomach and tightened its grip as I abandoned my search for soup to open the door leading from the garage into the kitchen. It was as I had feared—the renters downstairs had left the door unlatched. The wind had caught the door and blown it up against the back wall of the house, breaking off one of the hinges. I had just repaired it three days ago.

Grabbing the handle, I gingerly closed the broken door, latching it securely. One more item to add to the growing list of things that would need to be repaired or replaced when the lease was up. It seemed the list of things that needed repairing or replacing was never-ending, and it seemed the lease was always up. Why couldn't anyone stay in one place for longer than three months?

The concrete floor bit the bottoms of my feet through my slippers as I padded back into the house. So much for turning up the thermostat. I'd left the door open when I went out to the garage, and the temperature in the kitchen was now colder than when I'd been searching for that errant can of soup. Abandoning that mission, I reached for the jar of peanut butter instead, but my fingers came up empty.

No peanut butter. No soup. If there was no milk in the fridge, I knew I was really in trouble.

I retrieved my phone from the other room, finger poised on speed dial as I returned to investigate the refrigerator. The jangling tones of a call attempting to connect were already sounding in my ear as my eyes located the empty spot where the milk carton usually sits. Closing the refrigerator door, I heard the voice of the last person on Earth I care to speak to.

"She's back, isn't she?"

I closed my eyes and resisted a shudder, overwhelmed by the knifelike assault of his words against my soul. "How did you know?" I responded, striving (but failing) to sound calm and in complete control.

"It's been over two years since you called me last, and it's been that long since the last time she materialized." He forced a chuckle and I shivered, not from the temperature, but from foreboding.

Every ghastly visit began with the disappearance of those three items—the soup, the peanut butter, and the milk. The idiosyncrasy would perhaps be laughable in any other apparition, by any other person it chose to haunt. But it always struck terror to my core, and she knew it. No matter how hard I tried to overcome it, to pretend it didn't bother me, somehow she always managed to push my buttons.

I gulped in a deep breath, attempting to still my galloping heart. Or at least wrangle it back into its normal rhythm. "What should I do?" I wheezed plaintively into the phone, noting rather abstractly that my whitened fingertips clutched it in a death grip.

"Breathe."

If I hadn't been strangling the phone so intensely, I'd have thrown it across the room. He knew how to push my buttons, too. There were reasons why we'd signed those divorce papers, and why we never contacted each other. Not all the fault was mine.

"Why are you really calling, Kath?"

Oh yeah, I hadn't actually pitched the phone through the kitchen window—much as I wanted to. I resented the reminder that I was the one who had initiated this call, and I resented even more the fact that he was the only person who could help me. "I don't know what to do."

He was my nemesis, the person I least wished to see under any circumstance. Ours was an unholy alliance. Yet I was forced to rely on him, and it rankled.

This was one demon I couldn't face alone.

"Greg?" Half of me hoped he'd given up, disconnected the call, and left me to fend for myself. The other half clung to the hope that he would be my lifeline.

"I'm here," he breathed into my ear. "What do you want me to say? What can I even do from here?"

Right. He now lived 200 miles away. Not far enough, in my opinion.

"I'm sorry, I shouldn't have called. This was a bad idea."

"No, Kathy, wait—" I disconnected the call. Mentally haranguing myself for being so stupid, I shoved both hands—phone includ-

Photo by Makail Duran on Unsplash

ed—into my sweater pockets, trudged back through the living room, and down the hall to the back bedroom.

It had always been Em's bedroom. It remained her room even now, three years after we'd lost her. I suppose I should have turned it into a guest bedroom, a craft and sewing room, a home office—or found a roommate and rented it out. But I could

never bring myself to do it. I lived in constant hope that she would return someday, and that everything would go back to normal.

Only—things had never been normal. Even before Greg had moved out, she was already slipping away. But that had been the final straw.

My sweet, darling Emily, already so pale and thin, stared back at me from beneath stringy black hair, her too-large eyes filled with accusation: "Dad's not coming back, is he?"

"Not this time," I had replied, unthinking. "He found a better proposition. We've been replaced."

The instant those words had escaped me, I regretted them. It was too late to take them back—the damage had already been done. Having lost my husband long before he actually left the house, that was the day I lost my daughter. By the time I'd returned to her room with a bowl of soup, a peanut butter sandwich, and a cup of cocoa, she had slipped away.

I hesitated in the hallway before pushing open the door—a vain attempt to prepare myself for whatever awaited on the other side. The last visitation had been brief, the damage somewhat minimal, but I suspected this one would—escalate. It should. It was my fault we lost her in the beginning, and it was only fair she seek retribution from me.

I placed a trembling hand on the mostly-closed door and gave it a gentle push. The hinges squeaked as it opened, and I made a mental note to oil them. Assuming I survived this encounter.

103

Tiny hairs on my arms sprang to attention and prickled the back of my neck. The window on the far wall had been cracked open, and on the desk below sat the missing food items from my kitchen. The air was freezing in here—no wonder the house had grown so cold. I sprinted to the window and closed it.

I turned to see a macabre figure appear in the doorway, blocking my exit. Startled, I jumped, stifling a scream. I barely recognized her—cavernous eyes peering through wisps of barely-there spider web strands. Once-luminous pale skin slung listlessly across her skeletal frame and I imagined that if I listened closely enough, I could hear her bones rattle.

This was a face only a mother could love.

As much as I loved this face, it was hard to look at. Or to smell. Malevolence radiated from—it—filling the room with a pungent odor that burned the back of my throat, causing my eyes to water. I glanced around, looking for a safe place to fix my gaze—or to breathe—and spied a small pile of bloody tissues sitting in one corner next to a filthy backpack.

Sighing, I resolved to be the grownup. "It's been a long time, Emily."

My resolve was met with silence.

I decided to try again. "Is everything okay? I miss you. I miss my little girl filled with sunshine and laughter. And life." Remorse welled up within me like anaphylactic shock, cutting off my air supply. Unable to speak any further, I simply stood and looked at her.

She stared listlessly back at me. Then she took a step forward, stumbled, and fell. I ran to her, noting for the first time that there was blood on her shoulder. I guess that explained the pile of tissues.

I peeled back her clothing to take a closer look at the wound. It was putrid with infection and—was that a gunshot? I wasn't certain, as I'm not a nurse or anything, but I did know that calling for emergency medical services could endanger her. So I could not call.

I groped in the pocket of my sweater and dialed Greg's number once again. Then I deleted it instead

of sending. I dialed 911, but deleted that too. Shoving the phone back in my pocket, I turned back the covers on Emily's bed and lifted her into it, resolved to make her as comfortable as possible.

Collecting the pilfered food from Em's desk, I made my way back out to the kitchen, re-adjusting the thermostat as I passed it. Disregarding the brilliant blue and red lights flashing outside the picture window, I flipped the switch on the kettle. Situations like these could only be remedied with a peanut butter sandwich, a bowl of soup, and a mug of hot cocoa. The rest, we could figure out later.

The Storyteller
Rob Burton

Rob was the winner of the January 2018 I.P. Short Story Contest

I lie in my bed. It is dark. Through my open window I can hear the sounds of the city. Sirens. The constant streams of traffic rumbling along the street below send vibrations through the building. The indistinct chatter of passersby. Occasionally, a scream rises into a firework crescendo. Shouts and yells punctuated by cracked voices yelling 'Fuck Off,' 'Cunt.' These are the aggressive words used by the drunks, the drugged and the dispossessed that roam the empty streets looking for taxis, sex or the opportunity to beat someone to a pulp.

This was my night - my City.

Sometimes, between 3 a.m. and 4 a.m., it gets quiet. Regularly, I hear the heavy-metal chatter of helicopter blades churning the air above my district. I got out of bed once and opened the curtains to look. There was nothing to see, just the rattle of the blades making the window panes tremble in their frames like leaves in a breeze. Then, as the machine clattered into the distance, the night would once more surrender to an uneasy silence.

At about 5 a.m., dawn comes crashing through the gap above my window ledge. Heavy-duty machinery and the shouts of men at work startle me into a dazed consciousness. Bins clanging like

Photo by Yiran Ding on Unsplash

timpani drums as someone empties them into the gaping maw of the Dennis Eagle truck as it purrs its satisfaction on the road below.

Sleep is impossible and I lie in the tangle of my duvet - tepid with evaporating sweat. As much as I try to snooze the sounds of the City gathering pace slowly energise me. Sometimes I feel like I am an empty battery and the City noisescape is my power source. Each clanging, banging, roaring, screaming sound recharging every cell in my body as half-asleep I listen to my City gain momentum.

By 7 a.m. I am bored enough with myself and my thoughts that I arise and think about breakfast. After doing the usual things in and around the bathroom I throw open the curtains and check out the kitchen. Please don't think Jamie or Nigella here. This may well be the City, but if you are thinking granite worktops and stainless steel, think again. My kitchen in this shit-for-brains flat that I rent off some Arabic holding company comprises a microwave oven, a toaster and a double-ring burner. I also have a sink and a table-top fridge.

The fridge is empty. This is its normal state of being. Although I check it every morning in some meaningless ritual, just in case I have broken the habit of a lifetime and have stocked it with good healthy breakfast stuff like yoghurt and orange juice. Inside, where these items should offer their sweet inducements to a fitter and healthy life, are three tins of cheap supermarket lager held together by a plastic cuff and a yellowing, cracked hunk of cheddar cheese.

In the cafe down the street, I opt for the cooked breakfast. When I say 'opt' this does not indicate that I made a choice or had a choice. The establishments I favour are the places where choice is limited. I don't like making choices. I like certainty, the sure bet, the 100% odds-on favourite. Here it is the Full English. Two sausages, two bacon rashers, two eggs, beans, tomatoes, hash browns, black pudding, fried bread and a mug of builders tea. £4.99, a bargain. Not for this cafe the choice of the francophone continental

105

breakfast of rolls and jam or the effete 'beignet', the 'croissant' or the 'pain au chocolat' with a chocolate sprinkled latte or the hot caffeine shot of the espresso.

I leave replete. Happy that the food I was ingesting would last well beyond the interminable lunch hour. This would preclude me from making some spurious choices about what sandwich I would choose. I wouldn't have to think about the many ubiquitous sandwich shops I could decide on in my search to select a sandwich. I didn't do lunch—too much to choose from.

Why would I want to 'do lunch' anyway? My life isn't like that. I do not structure my days into distinct time zones like most of the clones on the street around me. The clock does not watch me and I do not watch the clock. In the City, time becomes irrelevant, geography is more important. It's where you are when things happen, not at what time they happen that's important.

Were you below the balcony when the cat knocked the plant pot off for it to fall six stories to smash into your head, killing you stone dead? Or did you stop for a latte in the new cafe around the corner? So missed the shattering of the geraniums on the pavement, the red petals scattering like scarlet bloodstains across the pavement instead of your brains. In the City things are happening all the time.

Every second of every day in the City there are dramas and tragedy. Lives are lived and lives are lost, fortunes rise and fortunes fade. In this City alone there are eight million stories every day. Johnson had it right when he opined 'for there is in London all that life can afford.' But for many of the citizens of this great City whilst all life they can afford might be available, for some it is just too expensive.

My job? I am the storyteller, the story maker. I am your fate and your fortune. I am death and I am life. I am war and I am peace. I can make you and break you. I am the silent disease and the roaring fire. I am peace. This is why I abhor choice. Why it is, in my life, if you can call it that, I go out of my way not to make choices? I cannot choose. In my

job I am obliged to make a thousand choices an hour, a million choices a day, an unfathomable number each year, each decade, each millennium. The choices stretch out like a carpet of nails, each choice pricking at me like a thorn on a rose bush.

This is my City. These are my people. I am theirs and they are mine.

I am nondescript as I walk through the City. I do not stand out. You might think I wear some mark, some sign that would single me out as the storyteller? A 666 tattoo perhaps? But I am not the Devil. Satan belongs in fiction. This is where he belongs at the right-hand side of God, Jesus, Mohammed, Buddha and the myriad of other characters these city dwellers believe answers their prayers, salves their guilt and smites their enemies. The so-called Holy Books of the religions, cults and sects act as panaceas to the stories I create. The stories I shape. These books attempt to explain the stories - they bulk out the script. They attempt to provide background and context. They give sense to the insensible, thought to the unthinkable, and add nothing to the nonsense, which is, after all, their lives.

I am not a Devil neither am I a God. I am a storyteller, the story maker. I have been telling stories since time began. I have been the maker and the breaker of men. From the lowly scribe to highest king I have made their stories. I have marked their path. But I am just one. This is my City. I am not omnipotent. That is fiction. I am not supernatural or a super being. I am not all things to everyone it is just I. One City - one storyteller.

For me to tell your story I have to cross your path. It can be a pure random chance that puts me in your vicinity. Maybe you missed your bus and get onto the next bus which is taking me across the city. Then you might sit next to me. As we brush arms, make even the slightest contact, I can tell your story. I can see your paths. I have to choose. It is my life - it is my burden.

I can see your past and I can see your futures. There are many and varied futures ahead of you. In that brief moment of contact I can see the intimate details of your life. I can see your hopes and fears, your loves and hates and all your dreams and ambitions. All there laid out in front of me as yet unfulfilled, untried, and to you unknown. I have to choose. I can tell your story. I can make your story.

I can make you rich or famous. I can guide you into the arms of your one true love. I can give you all you have ever wanted and I can take it all away. I can give you death. I have to make choices. I make the choices in that briefest fleeting moment of contact. I give you a story. It is yours and yours alone.

I wander through the City through the famous parks to the tourist destinations and onwards into the financial centre. I am a man in a crowd, a walker, and a stroller. You do not see me. I am anonymous. I fit in. You do not have to be a resident of the City either for me to tell your story. Tourists and visitors, should I encounter them, will take their stories back to Boise, Idaho, Nanjing, China, or Sydney, Australia. They will carry their story, their future back with them. Maybe they will encounter other storytellers en-route who will change my story; I cannot tell.

Neither do I discriminate against the rich or poor, black or white, male or female; they all have stories that need to be written. I do not hate. Hate is a fruitless emotion. Hate shrivels stories; it negates the spirit and closes the mind. My traverse through the City is random and spurious. I might wander around the markets, enjoying the sights and sounds of the traders and the banter.

As I walk, I nudge elbows and bump shoulders, thus I tell the stories. Here a child is written for a barren wife. Now a silent and cold lonely death. A fortune on a lottery ticket or a sudden and inexplicable illness. I choose these fates. It is not luck or magic or the result of chanting mantras to deities. These are in my gift; they are in my hands. They are yours. I give them to you.

I have my favourite places. Places where I have moved and told stories and given stories over the millennia. I sit down by the river where once I chose the stories for the Roman legionaries. I rest, away from people, one of the few times I try to exercise choice over my life. I take some respite from the stories and the choices. Sometimes even a storyteller needs quiet contemplation. Sometime I need time out. Time to watch the river flow and the grass grow. So many stories so many choices.

But I have a job to do. A storyteller cannot sit on his laurels for too long. I leave the quiet of the riverbank and walk to the Underground. This is fertile ground for a storyteller. So many people, so much jostling, so many elbows and shoulders, so many choices. I stay on the train as it circles my City. Sometimes I change trains; sometimes I stand and let the tides of humanity swirl around me. I watch people's lives. I read the lines. I change their futures. I make choices.

I am standing on a train when death touches me.

I see death, I feel death, and I smell death. I stand hanging on the rails surrounded by people. Barely touching me to my right is a man with a backpack on. He looks into my eyes and I see death. His story is a very short story. The ending is barely five minutes away. The train lurches, people sway. A woman to my left bumps against me. I see her story and the choices I can make for her. Should she get off at the next station? She has a newly discovered old friend who lives nearby. They will pick up their friendship. They will travel. They will have adventures. They will live together into old age, happy and contented. Or should she stay on to visit her new lover, she will be full of excitement and sexual tension but would die very shortly in agony and flames?

The rest of the carriage is packed, it's rush hour, I couldn't see their stories, I couldn't involve myself with everyone. There is just me. I am the storyteller. The man with the backpack lurches back against me. I change his story to one where he lives a long and happy life with his wife and daughter and to the woman on my left I give many afternoons of hot sexual passion. This will make her happy.

I look again at the man on the right with the backpack. He stares me in the eyes. I see the sweat on his brow. As I look I see him relax, I see the tension and death drain out of him. I smile at him. He smiles back. I touch him on the arm I see his story played out before me, the one I had just written. The train stops. We look at each other; something passes between us, but he cannot know what, he nods and gets off the train and walks away into his new story.

I walk through the carriage and deliberately bump into everyone. To each I give a gift. To the office secretary a reprieve from the cancer she doesn't yet know is growing inside her. To the lonely man an unexpected holiday romance, to the student struggling at university a successful career and so it goes through the carriage. It is in my behest to do this. I am not the grim reaper that takes away. I can be the joyful giver if I so wish. Another choice I can make in my life.

I leave the underground station wondering at man's inhumanity to man. Over the millenniums I have been the storyteller in my City. I have been witness to and have written some of the darkest of deeds. Man has free will. This is not something that some divine being has gifted to man. This is where I wrote Darwin's story, so he could tell us as part of his wondrous gift that men will always follow their strongest instincts which might prompt him to the noblest deeds but it will far more commonly lead him to gratify his own desires at the expense of other men.

So I might change the course of history for some. But I do not do it for all people. On my random meanderings around the city I change stories, but the base character of some men and women can and will act against my best efforts to tell the whole story. Someone once said, 'Men make their own history' and yes I agree in the main they do. But it is the storytellers that make the futures.

Take the man known as Jack the Ripper - a well-known serial killer of myth and mystery. His identity still unknown, still hidden and yet I gave him his story. He was just another random encounter. When he brushed against me that day in Whitechapel he was a struggling medical student with ambitions to be a surgeon. I remember that day as a good day: there were many good stories. I saw his stories. In one I saw the death and the anger and the resent-

ment. In the other I saw a good man. A pillar of the community, a loving father, destined to become a skilled surgeon. This is the story I gave him. But his base desires got the better of him. The story I gave him was played out as written but he added his own chapters, he created his own history as I had created his future. There was nothing I could do. I walked the streets of Whitechapel changing the dark stories of many of the low women I came across. But I am not the saviour. I am not omnipotent and some women, the women I missed, had to live their own stories and suffer those terrible endings.

Sometimes I wonder what I am. I am the storyteller. I have always been the storyteller. At the beginning I told the story and I will tell the story of the end. Time has no resonance. Time is only the passing of a summer breeze. This is my City. These are my people. I tell their stories. I make their choices.

As the shadows lengthen and the day slows into the shadowy evening, I join the groups of men, smoking short butts, toting scruffy military Bergens and sleeping bags, shuffling together sharing cans of Special Brew by the religious places. I try to keep my distance. I know their stories. These men have made their histories and I am not sure I want to give them a future story. These are difficult times for me. Giving stories is my job. It is not my job to discriminate, to shy away from contact. To not make stories. To let them pass. But I come here each evening.

I stand apart. But some of these men are long acquaintances. They see me and nod a friendly hello. In their small groups a few words are spoken and faces will be turned towards me. Sometimes one or two will drift over and say a few words. I offer cigarettes careful not to touch or be touched. I carry the cigarettes for their benefit not mine.

I know from long experience that contacts with military men and women or ex-military men and women are the most difficult for the storyteller. These men and women have been places and seen things that make even the most conscientious storytellers job impossible. When touched I am bombarded by the sights and sounds of war, death, destruction and mayhem. This has always been the case with warriors. They make their own stories. They make their own histories. They have no need of the storyteller and even if I were to give them the rosy future, they believe someday will be theirs, somehow, it always crumples into dust and despair. This is the weight they carry and will always carry for doing the dark work of the politicians.

Later, I enter the hall provided by a charity. They provide food for these homeless men and women. The room smells of sweat and cabbage, tobacco and beer. It smells of loneliness and camaraderie. The harsh lights bleach out the haggard and harried faces around me. I sit to one side. Once the queue for food had dropped, I take my place. There is no choice. I accept whatever food is placed upon my plate. I take a mug of hot tea, careful not to make contact with the good people that provide this service. Once again I shy away from telling their stories. I wonder how or why I make this choice.

Are there other storytellers? I don't know. Maybe. The world is a big place. There are billions of stories, billions of people making choices every day. Some have no choice in what they choose, for them it is written by their chance encounter with a storyteller. For others life is as mundane as it is written. Some people pray to gods and deities for a better life and for succour from the hardships they are facing. Some people sacrifice animals and humans hoping that the hot blood they release will feed the altruistic behaviour in some ravenous divinity living in some unknown dimension. These people are deluded. Only the storyteller can change things, only the storyteller has the keys to the future.

Late at night I return to my flat. I am tired. I have made many choices. Some will bloom like petals on flowers as the summer sun warms its buds to please all who come across it. Some will wither and die and cause distress and pain. Sometimes the story is too powerful for me to change. Sometimes a future is too dark for me to lighten and re-write. This is my burden. I sit in a sagging overstuffed chair. I watch the oblong of my window become opaque and darken as the light leaks out of the sky.

The sounds of the night drift through my window. Sirens and shouting, laughter and curses as I crack open the tin of cheap lager from my fridge and take a deep draught. As I swallow, I wonder again what my story might be.

The Contributing Writers

Tom Ashton
Tom is a novelist and short story writer from Barrow in Furness, Cumbria, UK, who holds a degree in Creative Writing from the University of Derby, has worked for both publishers and literary agencies, and is regularly asked to speak at Universities and Literature Festivals about his career.

Neil Austin
Neil, a house painter by trade, began to write in his 50s with a tale posted in episodes to Facebook. That story, and the world it created, gathered a few hundred fans. Reader feedback encouraged him to publish. With some editing and expansion, the Kala Bear Wars became his first book. Neil continues to write short stories and has a new novel in process.

Stephanie Neese
Stephanie is new to the horror genre and is the writer and producer of 'The Arcane Horror Podcast'. She lives with her husband and two dogs in the mountains where she enjoys listening to her favorite classic radio show: "Suspense!". When she isn't reading a good book or listening to the radio she can often be found hiking in the woods near her home, enjoying her time with nature. She finds inspiration for her stories in both her dreams, and her nightmares.

Imran Khan Bhayo
I am from the Sindh Province, the village of Karan Sharif near the city of Shikarpur in Pakistan. I am a police officer, but love to read and write. I write about true social issues and matters I see on the job, which destroy humanity. "A Mother killed & Burnt" is the first part of a novel, based on a true story I have written.

Rob Burton
Dr. Rob Burton is a writer, academic and ESL teacher. He has been living and teaching in China for over six years. He is the author of two novels, a novella, a racy memoir of 5 years in China (under a pen name – you will have to ask him), three ESL textbooks, plus he has written for academic journals, newspapers and magazines internationally. He lives on campus with his Chinese wife, 4 fish tanks (her's) Snook Doggy Dog, a Jack Russell bitch who came with him from the UK and a new kitten called Smokie – Snooky is not that pleased.
Find him at www.rob-burton.co.uk
www.Facebook.com/robburtonauthor

Benoit Chartier

Benoit is a Canadian author who shares his time between his home country and Japan, that of his wife. He is a writer of sci-fi, fantasy, paranormal, children's books, and philosophy. He also co-writes a podcast and voice-acts in it. He believes that education and love are the two most important things to change the world.

Cyan Ciar

Cyan was born in Tucson, Arizona, but his parents moved him to Omaha, Nebraska when he was two years old due to medical complications. Six years later, when his parents divorced, his mother moved to Oklahoma to live with his grandparents. He came out as transgender and pansexual when he was 16, and is currently engaged to his partner of four years. Cyan wants to become a novelist and have an LGBT+ character in every story he publishes.

Joanna Dwyer

Joanna has been an avid writer for over twenty years and has had many non-fiction essays published, as well as her debut book; Confessions of Butterflies: Hidden Truths of Living in Pain. Though she is a diverse writer, In The End is her first published piece of fiction. Joanna spends her days grooming dogs and her evenings scribbling away.

Eddie Eichelberger

Some people call him a Space Cowboy; some call him a misanthropic social misfit. Eddie likes long walks on the beach, cuddling underneath a blanket in front of a fire, and aggressively tailgating slow drivers. When he's not contemplating the mysteries of the Universe, you can find him walking aimlessly, mumbling under his breath—most likely rehearsing an argument he's already lost in case it comes up again. He lives and works in central Pennsylvania but aspires to be homeless in Santa Monica.

M.T. Finnberg

M.T. believes fiction helps us imagine how the world could be—maybe even how to make it a better place. M.T. is an absolute sci fi and fantasy nut. After a career as a psychologist, she tries to find the time for writing while building up her small business as a life coach and reiki healer, and spending time with her two awesome kids. In her spare time, she can be found cross-country skiing with her phone in one hand (you have to make notes when those plot twist ideas pop into your head, right!?), trying out vegan recipes, drinking too much coffee, and playing chauffeur to her kids.

Ayo Gutierrez

Ayo is an author, TV host, and professional speaker. Her poetry is inspired by the life that surrounds her, as well as the everyday human trials and tribulations that she comes across. She believes that she must give back to life what she has been taking from it all these years—and to do so, she has chosen to share her poetry with the world.

Ayo is the author of: *Buy 1 Fake 1*, *Bards from the Far East*, and *Yearnings*.

Hannah Ifeoluwa

Faleti Hannah I. is an upcoming poet and writer from Nigeria. Her work depicts the societal problems of her country and the solutions to them. Currently she is studying law in the highly-respected Obafemi Awolowo University in Ile-Ife, Nigeria. Her dream is to become an advocate for the voiceless and to touch many lives.

Rebecca Kapjon

Becky lives in Chicago, IL. She is a mother of two daughters and enjoys spending as much time as she can with her family. Becky has always been an avid reader and enjoys many different genres, so she decided to write her own stories. She is a huge Disney fan and loves everything *Harry Potter* along with loving cheering on her favorite sports teams especially the Bears (football) and Blackhawks (Hockey).

KMJVB

Person of crazy cool nothing, trips, rips, all those horrible feelings, But...good ones too, in your periphery, that's me. Horrible romantic realist: KMJVB

Corrie Lavina Knight

Corrie writes food for thought as science fiction, poetry, songs, and scripts for live theatre production. An avid songwriter and singer who loves hot beverages and all things creative, this Canadian American resides with her husband in Montana, USA. One day she might audition for one of those reality-TV talent shows to see if she has what it takes to pursue a career in music but until then, she will find other reasons to take extended road trips. With friends and family members who live on every continent (including Antarctica), she still has a lot of ground to cover.

Jeremy Morang

Jeremy lives in Central Maine. He is married, and a father to two daughters. He works with adults with physical and cognitive disabilities and has been involved in that line of work for eight years. In his off time, he writes, reads, and tries to make a better life for his family. He enjoys the company of friends, a strong cup of coffee, a raging bonfire, listening to classic rock and day trips to the coast.

Bryan Oliphint

Bryan lives and works in Southeast Texas. In his spare time, he relishes coffee, hopes for nightmares, and enjoys writing psych horror and dark poetry. He is happily married and has two college-aged boys, as well as two four-legged mutts.

Edentu Oroso

Edentu is a biographer, poet, essayist, magazine columnist, novelist, and Public Speaker. He's the author of *Tears From a Rose; The Alfa Sky*, a biography of Air Marshal Ibrahim Mahmud Alfa - Nigeria's longest serving Chief of Air Staff; *Wings of Freedom*, a biography of Ralph Igbago - former Deputy Speaker Benue State House of Assembly, Nigeria; and *Songs of the Gilded Penunder* the pen name Dean Max

S.L. Ramero

S.L. is a writer out of Lake Jackson, TX, where he lives with a family that assists his fight against dragons, demons, and angry senior citizens. Oftentimes he fights the zombie apocalypse alongside his canine companion, Ser Ghost. But every night as he's lying down, he contemplates whether he's had enough sleep or not. And shit hasn't hit the fan...YET.

Michael Recto

Michael works as a spreadsheet master by profession and plays video games to un-wind. He is also an anime fan and a day dreamer for as long as he could remember. And yeah, he's also a writer. If he's not out like a light catching up on his REM cycles during the weekends, he runs like a lunatic through the endless fields of words, desper-ately chasing them down and splicing them together into chimeras of poems and short stories. You can follow him through his social media sites at: Facebook: https://www.facebook.com/mogerus/, Instagram: recto.michael
Twitter: @mogerus.
You can also check his websites at: Wordpress: michaelrecto.wordpress.com
Wattpad: www.wattpad.com/user/mogerus

M.E. Shao

Afflicted by rhythm, his thoughts are in rhyme. You'll find that he writes almost all of the time. If scribbling he isn't, he's either cutting a log—or walking the trails with his super cool dog.

Randall Thompson

I live, work and write from my home in beautiful rural Nova Scotia, Canada. Writing novels, short stories, poems and essays has been a part of my life for as long as I can remember. Sharing those creations—my characters, and their wild adventures with others, has become my passion. Although my eccentric characters and their miscre-ant tales are all works of fiction, a thread of truth is woven through each story. I write what I see, what I know and the old legends I've been told. Since the time we lived in caves, the telling of stories has been at the very heart of what it is to be human. I enjoy the humorous, the dramatic and the bizarre. My readers never know what to expect next, because in one of my stories…anything is possible.

Tissy Taylor

Tissy began writing as soon as she could hold a crayon. Born the middle of three children, she was raised in Ontario, Canada. She found her writing voice early on, serving two community newspapers as a family columnist and recently published her first poetry collection "Madness, Chaos Unravelled". She currently works as a Senior Business Analyst and Communications Manager.

Jai Thoolen

Jai is a large, nearly 40-year-old, Australian man who writes children's books and poetry. He is still a child at heart and that shows in some of his writing. Author of 'My Beard', 'My Safe Word Is Poetry' and several more. He has also contributed to several anthologies and can be found at picklepoetry.com or on Amazon. Follow him on social media platforms @picklepoetry.

M Lynn Valle

Who IS M Lynn?...this writer from southern Michigan?...I will show you through words. I am an author of poetry, unfiltered. I write of life that involves my surroundings and thoughts...all you have to do is READ.

Abigail Wild

As a graphic designer, writing instructor, and artist, Abigail has found that writing gives her a sense of peace. Often described as having her head in the clouds, she writes to reveal a connection between Earth and sky, reality and fantasy, pain and hope. Current writing projects include: *Shattered Self* (her debut novel), pursuing an MFA in creative writing, and working with emerging writers.

About Trode Publications

Trode Publications is a small press with large aspirations. This is its first opportunity to publish an anthology of diverse authors, and we are eager to see how this eclectic, international bunch of talented people will be received on the world stage.

If you've read this far...

It would be of tremendous help, both to the contributing writers featured in this anthology as well as to Trode Publications, if you would consider logging on to Amazon and penning a review of our collective effort.

"And by the way, everything in life is writable
if you have the outgoing guts to do it, and the imagination to improvise.
The worst enemy to creativity is self-doubt."

— Sylvia Plath

www.ingramcontent.com/pod-product-compliance
Lightning Source LLC
Chambersburg PA
CBHW081147170626

46809CB00010B/3121